rhcbooks.com

ISBN 978-0-593-31063-2 (hardcover) — ISBN 978-0-593-31064-9 (paperback)
— ISBN 978-0-593-31065-6 (ebook)

Printed in the United States of America
10 9 8 7 6 5 4 3 2 1

JURASSIC WORLD
DOMINION

THE JUNIOR NOVELIZATION

Adapted by David Lewman

Random House 🏠 New York

CHAPTER ONE

On a moonlit night, two hooded figures cut the links of a barbed-wire fence surrounding an industrial farm. They squeezed through the opening, stealthily crossed the yard, and slipped into a large metal barn.

They didn't like what they found inside.

Claire Dearing stared angrily at the rows of baby *Nasutoceratops* crammed into small cages. Each *Nasutoceratops* resembled a baby rhino with a solid frill behind its head, a mouth like a parrot's beak, and two horns. The creatures were cute but miserable.

Zia Rodriguez immediately pulled out her phone and began filming the cages. "We're inside an illegal breeding facility," she narrated in a hushed voice. "The juveniles are raised in cages to keep down costs."

In a rolling cage, one of the *Nasutoceratops* groaned. *MMMRRR*. Zia checked its pulse and shined a penlight into its eye. "He's not looking good," the paleoveterinarian said.

Feeling rage building inside her, Claire stated, "We can't leave him here." She started to pick the lock on the dinosaur's ankle cuff.

"Claire, no," Zia protested. "We can report this."

"The Department of Fish and Wildlife takes days to investigate," Claire argued. "We can save this one now."

Soon they were rolling the heavy cage down an unpaved road just outside the fence. Back near the barn, security guards with flashlights shouted something about intruders. The baby *Nasutoceratops* made a braying sound.

"*Shhh,*" Claire whispered, trying to soothe it. "Okay, *shhh.*"

A van backed up to them. Franklin Webb opened the rear doors from inside and saw Claire and Zia cradling the moaning *Nasutoceratops.* "This was not the plan," he said nervously.

Claire slipped into the driver's seat and drove the van down the rough road as Zia and Franklin bounced around in the back. Zia tried to sedate the baby dinosaur. Spotting a pickup truck coming after them, Claire hit the gas. "Hang on!" she cried. *VROOM!*

Turning off the road, Claire crashed through a gate and drove across bumpy ground.

"It's okay," Franklin told the *Nasutoceratops.* "Just going for a little ride."

THOMP! The dinosaur thrashed and kicked. The van shook and the back door flew open! The truck was right behind them, driven by a woman who looked furious at having her valuable property stolen. A man leaned out the passenger window and fired a shotgun, aiming for the van's tires. He hit the bumper instead. *BLAM! TINK!*

"Claire, we're gonna get shot!" Zia yelled.

Dead ahead, Claire spotted a full-grown *Triceratops* and swerved around it. The truck tried swerving, too, but tipped over and landed on its side. *WHAM!*

They got away, and Zia finally managed to inject the sedative. "There you go. Nap time."

"Everybody good?" Claire called back from the driver's seat.

"NO!" Franklin and Zia shouted in unison.

By sunrise, they were driving down an empty road with the baby dinosaur peacefully sleeping in the back.

"Okay," Claire said. "So I think we should get this one to safety and then hit that facility again."

"Whoa, whoa," Franklin said, shaking his head. "Look, we'll get this one to the Department of Fish and Wildlife and make sure she's safe. But after that, we can't do this anymore."

"You're quitting?" Claire asked, surprised.

"Quitting what?" Franklin asked. "This isn't an actual organization anymore."

Claire looked disappointed. She still felt terrible about her role in the disaster at Jurassic World. Trying to save the dinosaurs that had escaped into North America and the world was the only way she knew how to make up for that.

Zia understood how Claire felt. "Look," she said. "You're responsible for something that hurt a lot of people. You want to fix it, but this is not the way to go about it."

"But they need us," Claire pleaded.

"Are you saving these dinosaurs because they need us?" Franklin challenged. "Or are you saving them to absolve yourself?"

Claire ignored his question. "A lot of people want these animals dead."

"Yeah," Franklin agreed. "And if people like us are in jail, they win. Last week I got offered a real job, something I can do to effectively change things. I've got to take it. I'm sorry."

"Claire," Zia said gently. "I know you want to do right by your past. But this isn't about you anymore."

Claire slowly nodded. She knew Zia was right. But that didn't make it any easier.

In the Sierra Nevada Mountains, a herd of juvenile *Parasaurolophuses* thundered across the open range, kicking up powdery snow. A man on horseback rode alongside the dinosaurs, rounding them up.

Owen Grady.

A woman named Rosa and a man named Shep rode nearby, helping drive the herd. Shep whistled, keeping the dinosaurs moving.

Suddenly, a *Parasaurolophus* broke away from the other dinosaurs and ran off on its own. Owen galloped after the rogue dinosaur, drew his lasso, and roped the runaway. But it kept on going, stomping down a rocky slope. Owen had to slide off his horse, holding on to the rope. He managed to wrap it around a tree stump and pull it taut to stop the *Parasaurolophus*.

"There you go," he said to the dinosaur, trying to calm the frightened animal. "*Shhh*. You're all right."

The creature was bucking wildly, but Owen kept speaking in his soothing voice until it settled down. Soon he was able to bring the *Parasaurolophus* back to the herd and slip the lasso off. It fell in step with its fellow dinosaurs, a member of the pack once again.

As the sun started to set, Owen, Shep, and Rosa led the herd across a shallow stream. Through the trees, Owen spotted a man on horseback. And then another. He could see shotguns in their hands. They whistled to each other. Soon four men on horseback had circled the herd of dinosaurs.

Owen frowned.

CHAPTER TWO

Owen looked up to the top of a hill and saw a pair of pickup trucks and more men on horseback, watching, ready to come down and help.

The leader of the four riders, a man named Delacourt, told Owen threateningly, "Poaching gets you three to five years in prison. You know that. Looks like we'll be taking this herd off your hands."

"On what authority?" Owen asked.

Opening his trench coat to show a patch sewn inside, Delacourt said, "Department of Fish and Wildlife."

"That's funny," Owen said, "because my friends here know all the new recruits." Rosa and Shep flipped their wallets open to show the gold badges identifying them as special agents with the Department of Fish and Wildlife. "Did you see these guys at orientation?" Owen asked them.

"Nope," Shep said.

7

Owen turned back to Delacourt. "So what's the going rate for *Parasaurolophus* bone powder now? Thousand dollars an ounce?"

"I'd say more like six or seven." Delacourt smirked.

Owen whistled. "So I'd say we've got about five hundred grand worth of dinosaur right here. But if it weren't for poachers like you, we'd let 'em run wild."

Delacourt pulled out a shotgun. Shep and Rosa drew their revolvers. "Hold it!" Rosa warned.

Up on the hill, Delacourt's men took aim. "How y'all want this to go?" Delacourt asked. "Your bones ain't worth nothing to me, but don't think I won't rip 'em out of you."

Delacourt's right-hand man, Wyatt, locked eyes with Owen. "He's not lying."

Owen knew they were seriously outnumbered and outgunned. He made a hard decision. "Take 'em," he said. "Go on."

Grinning, Delacourt and his men herded the dinosaurs up the hill to the trucks. "See you around," Delacourt called back over his shoulder.

When the rustlers were gone, Shep said to Owen, "Never seen you walk away from a fight."

Several conflicting feelings flashed through Owen's eyes, but he only replied, "I got obligations."

Thirteen-year-old Maisie Lockwood finished stacking firewood alongside a mountain cabin. She hopped on her bike, popped in her earbuds, and rode off through the snow toward a small logging town.

From the woods, a *Velociraptor* watched her pedaling fast down the road. The raptor was named Blue. Years earlier, she'd been named and trained by Owen. She watched Maisie ride by but left the girl alone.

At the town's bait shop, Maisie set lures, fishing hooks, and a flashlight on the counter. As the store's owner rang up the items, she asked, "Shouldn't you be in school?"

"It's fine," Maisie assured her. "I'm homeschooled."

"That so," the owner said skeptically.

Heading back home, Maisie cut through the lumber yard. Work had stopped because a pair of huge, gentle *Apatosauruses* had wandered into the mill. The workers didn't know what to do. Maisie made a suggestion to the foreman. He took it, telling one of his workers to light a flare and climb onto the back of a water truck. The foreman drove the truck away, and the dinosaurs followed it out of the mill. Work resumed, thanks to Maisie's insight into dinosaur behavior.

When Maisie got back to the cabin, Claire was outside burning her clothes and a blanket from the raid on the industrial farm in a steel drum. She wanted to get rid of any evidence that she, Franklin, and Zia had broken in and rescued a baby *Nasutoceratops*.

"Hey," Claire called to Maisie, spotting snow on her jacket. "Where have you been?"

"Nowhere," Maisie fibbed. "What are you burning?"

"Nothing," Claire said, telling a fib of her own. "Just some old blankets. You sure you didn't go past the bridge?"

"Nope," Maisie said. "You sure those are old blankets?"

"Yep," Claire claimed. The two looked at each other, each waiting for an admission.

"That's the look you get when you think I'm lying," Maisie said.

"Are you?" Claire asked.

"No."

"You're kind of looking everywhere but here."

"I'm not."

"Yeah, you're completely avoiding eye contact."

"I said I didn't go past the bridge!" Maisie barked, grabbing a piece of firewood and stomping off into the cabin.

Claire followed her in and found Maisie adding the log to the cabin's woodstove. "Can we start over?"

Claire asked. She hadn't meant to make Maisie angry.

"I know, I know—there are people who will do anything to find me," Maisie said, having heard it a thousand times.

"Yeah, but that doesn't mean you can't do fun stuff, like—"

"Feed the goats?" Maisie asked, interrupting her. "Mix compost? These things are not fun."

"Hey, I'm not angry," Claire said. "That means you don't have to be angry."

"I'm not angry!" Maisie insisted, slamming the stove's door shut. *CLANK!* "I want to go out for pizza. And bowling. Why can't we do that?"

"You know why," Claire said quietly.

"So you're gonna hide me here forever?" Maisie asked. "Watching the same six DVDs over and over?"

"We're trying to keep you safe," Claire explained.

"I can take care of myself, Claire," Maisie said, storming into her room.

Claire followed her. "It's okay for us to depend on each other," Claire said. "That's what people do."

Maisie wheeled around to face Claire. "How should I know what people do? The only people I've talked to in the past four years are you both. I'm not a real person anyway."

Claire looked shocked.

CHAPTER THREE

"**W**hat?" Claire asked.

"I'm not . . . me," Maisie said. The unspoken truth was that Maisie was a clone, created from the DNA of Benjamin Lockwood's daughter. Though she knew it wasn't strictly true, Maisie still thought of Benjamin Lockwood as her grandfather, and she missed him and her old life.

"Oh, honey," Claire said, her heart breaking at Maisie's statement. "You're the only one who ever was."

Maisie tried not to cringe, but Claire knew she had gone too far.

"That was corny, wasn't it?" Claire asked.

"It was super corny," Maisie said as the tension dissipated.

"Please don't tell anyone," Claire asked.

"I can't promise that," Maisie said, smiling. Headlights flashed in the window. Maisie's smile got even bigger. "Owen!" She ran out of the cabin to greet him.

As Owen closed the truck door, Maisie hugged him. "Hey, kid," he said affectionately. He hugged her back. "Sorry I'm late."

Maisie wrinkled her nose. "You smell like horses."

"Mmm," Claire said, agreeing.

"Do you like that?" Owen asked her.

"I do," Claire said. As she and Owen started to kiss, Maisie quickly slipped back inside the cabin, saying, "I'm gonna make dinner." She had no interest in watching her guardians kiss.

"Everything good?" Owen asked.

Claire's lips tightened. "She went into town again."

Owen furrowed his brow. "You talk to her?"

"I tried," Claire said, shrugging.

In the pine forest, the raptor named Blue watched Owen and Claire. Then she took off through the woods, nimbly darting between trees and bushes, making her way back to an abandoned school bus covered in moss. The bus had been rusting away in the same spot for fifty years.

13

Blue entered through a gaping hole in the side of the bus. Inside, an old tire lined with dirty rags held the broken shell of a dinosaur egg.

A four-foot raptor cautiously emerged from its hiding place in the bus. She looked exactly like her larger mother. Blue screeched and led the way out of the bus. Her daughter followed her.

Snow fell in the woods. Blue and her young offspring stalked a rabbit. Just as they were about to pounce, a wolf exploded from the bushes and ate the rabbit. Blue screeched, and her daughter lunged at the wolf, biting its shoulder.

BLAM! A bullet hit the snow inches from the young raptor. She scrambled away, confused. Blue spotted two game hunters wearing white camouflage. One cocked his gun. *CLICK.*

Blue leapt toward them. *BLAM!* The bullet landed just behind her. The raptor made quick work of the two hunters. They never stood a chance.

Owen looked toward the woods when he heard the gunshots, concerned for Blue.

"You okay?" Claire asked.

"Hunting season," Owen said.

Later that night, Maisie, Owen, and Claire sat outside the cabin, enjoying a roaring campfire. Owen sharpened his knife while Maisie whittled a stick with hers.

"How old were you when you got your first knife?" Maisie asked.

"Older than you," he said. "Always cut away from yourself."

Maisie gave him an annoyed look, feeling as though he was being overprotective again. Owen noticed and decided to shift gears. He flipped his knife in his hand.

"Come here," he said. "Remember what I told you about fighting with a knife? Get your forearm up. Target the weak spots." He made quick stabbing motions. "One, two. Then, while they're bleeding out, say something cool like 'Wrong girl, wrong time.'"

"Wrong girl, wrong time," Maisie said, trying to sound cool.

"Okay, good," Owen said, "but more . . . dangerous."

"Wrong girl. Wrong time," Maisie growled in a low voice.

"That was stone-cold," Owen said, impressed.

"Yeah, I wouldn't mess with you," Claire agreed.

Pleased, Maisie flipped her knife around in her hand, copying Owen's move. The two adults looked startled. "No!" they both said at the same time.

But she'd caught the knife without cutting herself. She shot them a look that said, "What?"

Owen decided a certain topic couldn't be put off any longer. "Maisie," he said, "we've got to talk about you going into town."

"It was only one time," Maisie protested.

"It only takes one time," Owen said.

"You don't realize what it's like to be trapped here."

"You're not trapped," Owen disagreed. "We just don't trust people."

"No, you don't trust *me*," Maisie complained. "And you expect me to trust you. Why can't I just have some freedom?"

"You just can't," Owen said firmly.

Maisie stormed off into the cabin.

"That went great," Owen said dryly to Claire.

"When did this happen?" Claire asked. "She was calling us Mom and Dad. Now all of a sudden, it's like she hates us."

"She doesn't hate us," Owen said, stirring the fire with a stick. "She's a teenager. Remember what that was like?"

"We can't keep her here forever," Claire said.

"Sure we can," Owen said unreasonably.

"If we don't figure this out, she'll go a lot farther than the bridge."

"If they find her, we'll never see her again," Owen insisted. "We've got to protect her. That's our job."

"Protect her how?" Claire asked. "By locking her inside? How much longer is that going to last?"

They both looked through the cabin's window, seeing Maisie's shadow move against the wall inside.

"She has questions we can't answer," Claire said. "She wants to know who she is. Who she was."

Inside, Maisie opened a trunk in her room and pulled out a photo album. It was filled with pictures of Benjamin Lockwood's dead daughter, Charlotte. Looking at dinosaur eggs in an incubator. Celebrating Christmas with scientists. Pointing up at the gates of Jurassic Park, excited. Leaving for college in a packed car.

Someone had stuck an old newspaper article in the album. The headline read CHARLOTTE LOCKWOOD AWARDED GRUBER PRIZE IN GENETICS.

Maisie stared at the pictures, trying to understand the identical twin she'd never met.

That same evening, the poacher, Delacourt, sat in his truck talking in a gruff but low voice on his phone.

"You were right," he said. "The raptor's got a juvenile. If you want it, it won't come cheap." As the person on the other end of the line named a very high figure, Delacourt smiled.

"Yeah, that'll do. Listen, there's something else," he said. "I found that girl you've been after."

CHAPTER FOUR

At dawn on a farm in West Texas, a girl named Alicia fed the chickens while her brother, Ramon, gathered eggs. As he brushed the straw off an egg, he noticed an enormous locust with spiked legs on a fence post. He'd never seen anything like it. As he stepped closer, a huge swarm of locusts rose from the wheat field past the fence into the sky!

Suddenly both kids were surrounded by a cloud of monstrous locusts! They ran into the barn and barely managed to close the door. Ramon spotted a locust inside the barn with them! Alicia slammed a bucket down to trap the bug. The bucket rattled and shook.

Later that day, a pickup truck drove up to the farm. The driver's door opened, and Dr. Ellie Sattler, a paleobotanist who had witnessed the tragic attacks at the original Jurassic Park, climbed out. Her two student assistants unloaded equipment.

Alicia and Ramon's dad, the farm's owner, stepped forward. "Wasn't sure who to call," he said by way of a greeting. "Fish and Wildlife didn't even want to see it if it wasn't a dinosaur."

"Yep, well, the dinosaurs get all the attention," Ellie said. She looked at the barn covered in locusts.

"They hit sixty fields in this county," the farmer continued. "You ever see anything like this before?"

Ellie shook her head. "Not like this. But these things have been ruining fields all across the Midwest." She climbed up on a tractor to get a better view of the farmer's ruined wheat field. She noticed that the next field over looked fine. "Is that your land?" she asked, pointing.

"That's the Bennetts'," he said.

"Do they plant the same seed as you?"

"No, we're independent. They use Biosyn seed."

"I bet they do," Ellie said, climbing down from the tractor. "You say you caught a live specimen?"

The farmer led the way into the house's living room, where Alicia and Ramon were feeding the locust celery through the sides of its rabbit cage. It yanked the stalks out of their hands forcefully.

"Wow, look at that," Ellie said. She leaned down to

examine the insect—a foot long and powerful, with yellow and red markings. She carefully took a saliva sample from its mouth and fed it into a DNA sequencer. When she saw the results, Ellie frowned. "I'm going to have to take this specimen back to my lab."

"Are you going to kill it?" Ramon asked.

"No," Ellie assured him. "I just need a second opinion. From an old friend."

At a dinosaur dig site in the West, a handsome, gray-bearded paleontologist named Dr. Alan Grant carved out the rock around the fossilized leg bone of a *T. rex*. Years before, he and Dr. Ellie Sattler had been invited to Jurassic Park by Dr. John Hammond before its official opening.

The visit had not gone well. At all . . .

Now Grant was trying to give a tour to paying visitors and their bored teenagers. As he showed them the fossil, a fifteen-year-old named Madison held out her phone. It was playing a video of a *T. rex* rampaging through a drive-in movie theater. "That's a *T. rex*," Madison said. "They've been around since the nineties. Why are we out here digging for bones?"

"You'd like to meet one of these, huh?" Grant said,

his anger building. If this girl had any idea what it was like to actually encounter a *T. rex* . . .

One of the other paleontologists coughed, subtly reminding Grant not to insult the tourists. The dig was largely paid for by their fees.

Grant calmed himself down. "Why do we dig?" he said, addressing the whole group. "Because science is about the truth. And there's truth in these rocks. Plus, it's a lot safer."

A nearby tourist called, "Dr. Grant, we found a fossil!"

He looked over and saw two tourists digging furiously and beckoning for him to come see their discovery. Grant ambled across the cavern, reached down, and pulled a plastic container up out of the dirt. "There you go," he said, handing it to them. "New species. Start thinking of a name."

Another paleontologist called out, "Grant! You're needed! Grant!"

Exhaling, Grant wiped his brow and looked up to the cavern entrance above. A young paleontologist was standing there, silhouetted against the bright sunlight behind him.

"You're going to want to see this," he called down.

CHAPTER FIVE

When he stepped into his cluttered tent full of books and fossils, Grant was surprised at what—who—he saw. "Ellie Sattler," he said.

"Alan Grant," Ellie said, smiling.

He hadn't seen her in years. "I don't know what to say."

"You look . . . the same," Ellie told him. "And this place is so you."

"Is it?" he said, a little flustered. "Sorry, if I'd known you were coming . . ." He moved a fossil or two, attempting to make the tent look a little neater, but instantly realized the impossibility of this. "Can I get you something?"

"Do you have iced tea?"

"Iced tea. Okay," Alan said, wondering if he had any tea. Or ice. Or glasses. "I can do that. I think."

Moments later, Alan poured from a hastily made jug of iced water with tea bags in it. He handed Dr.

Sattler a glass. Taking it, she said, "I saw you letting those kids have it down there."

"Tourists," he said, shaking his head. "Funding's all dried up. Something's got to pay for all this."

After they had caught up a bit, Ellie showed Alan the locust specimen, lifting its cage onto his desk and removing a cloth cover. The insect's wings fluttered, making a dry, rustling sound.

Alan leaned in, staring at the huge bug. "It's massive. Thorax, wings, mandibles—all like a modern locust."

"Yes," Sattler agreed. "But it has genes that have been extinct since the Cretaceous Period. I've been tracking this swarm since January. It started as a few hundred insects, but there could be millions by the end of summer. The damage is catastrophic. If it keeps up, there won't be enough grain to feed chickens or cattle. The entire food chain would collapse."

Examining the locust, Grant said, "It's got to be designed by human scientists. But why would anyone do that?"

"None of the crops these insects are eating come from Biosyn seed," Ellie told him.

Grant watched the grinding motion of the locust's powerful jaws as it ate celery. *CRUNCH. CRUNCH.* "You're saying Biosyn made this?"

"It doesn't shock me that they'd want to control the world's food supply."

"But not before a few million people starve." Alan touched the locust through the cage with a pencil. It fluttered its wings and slightly changed in color. It looked magnificent and scary at the same time. "Have you taken this to the Department of Agriculture?"

"Biosyn Genetics practically runs big agriculture these days," Ellie said, shaking her head. "No, this needs to go public, all at once."

Grant looked up from the insect. "So why are you bringing it to me?"

Ellie leaned forward and lowered her voice. "I need concrete evidence. I need to get to Biosyn's facility and extract a DNA sample from another locust there. But I need a witness: you. You command respect. People believe you."

Sighing, Alan stood and took a step away, thinking, scratching his gray beard. Then he turned back and said, "Ellie, you know why I'm out here in the middle of nowhere on this dig. It's quiet. I'm done with taking on the powers that be. I like being out of the spotlight, doing my own work. The work I love."

Ellie moved toward him. "I get it. I do. But none of us has that luxury anymore. Not even you. And you know what? You're the one I truly trust."

Alan reconsidered. When someone you respected put their trust in you, it was hard to say no. But he still wasn't absolutely convinced Ellie's plan was feasible.

"Biosyn Valley is five hundred miles from anything. How would you even get in?"

Dr. Sattler grinned. "I got an invitation. A week ago. From their in-house philosopher." When Alan looked puzzled, Ellie pulled a book out of her backpack. It was called *How the World Will End*. On the back of the book was a picture of its author, Dr. Ian Malcolm.

Grant grimaced slightly. He remembered Dr. Ian Malcolm all too well. Ian, Ellie, and Alan had been the three experts John Hammond had brought in to preview Jurassic Park. Malcolm struck Grant as arrogant and a little smarmy.

"Turns out there's a lot of money in being a chaotician these days," Ellie explained. "That's why Ian's at Biosyn."

"Chaotician," Grant said. "I still can't believe that's a real title. So he just invited you out of the blue? That sounds deeply suspicious to me."

Ellie shrugged. "He said there were some things I'd want to see."

"Uh-huh," Grant grunted skeptically.

"So," Sattler said, "what do you say? Are you in, Dr. Grant?"

Alan eyed the enormous locust in its cage. Then he looked at Ellie. "You know," he said, "when people talk me into these kind of things, it can get . . . messy." He was thinking of what had happened when John

Hammond had talked him into inspecting Jurassic Park. People had died. He, Ellie, and Ian Malcolm had been lucky to escape with their lives.

"Sometimes science is messy," she said. "Sometimes life is messy. But we don't want it to end because some big greedy company invented a deadly pest and we didn't do anything to stop them."

Grant slowly nodded. "Okay," he said, making up his mind. "Let the mess begin."

CHAPTER SIX

At a US Department of Fish and Wildlife facility in Pennsylvania, a sedated *Tyrannosaurus rex* in a cage was being lifted into a large airplane. Ellie and Alan watched the loading of the *T. rex* as they were guided across the airfield by a Department of Fish and Wildlife trainee named Shira. The plane's hatch closed, revealing the name **BIOSYN** stenciled on the door.

Over the deafening roar of the airplane's engines, Shira shouted, "Every animal captured on the mainland comes through here before they fly to Biosyn Genetics in the Dolomite Mountains. We give them medical attention and make sure they leave healthy."

Noticing a pair of heavily armed Biosyn guards, Ellie said, "This is quite an operation."

Shira grinned. "Those are just the guards you can see. There are a lot of shady types out there who want these dinosaurs." They reached a gate in a fence. "Can you please look in that camera for a second?"

Alan and Ellie looked at the camera. The gate unlocked. *CLUNK.* Shira stepped through, and the scientists followed her into the fenced enclosure. In the distance, they could see their plane waiting.

"Your plane's just fueling up," Shira said. "Biosyn's a tough invite. You must know somebody."

They passed an open pen full of baby *Nasutoceratops,* including the one Claire had rescued from the industrial farm with Zia and Franklin. Even though dinosaurs had been walking the earth again for decades, the sight of them still took Ellie's breath away.

"Do you mind if I take a look?" she asked.

Shira nodded. Ellie knelt to see the *Nasutoceratops* eye to eye.

"We rescued these guys from an illegal breeding farm in Nevada a few weeks ago," Shira explained. "Shut the whole thing down. Received an anonymous tip."

Ellie pulled a small flashlight from her pocket and clicked it on. When she moved the flashlight in front of one of the *Nasutoceratops'* eyes, it followed the light curiously. Ellie smiled, charmed by the sturdy little creature.

Inside the Biosyn cargo plane, Grant and Ellie found two seats next to each other among the crates. Grant struggled with his complicated multistrap seat belt. Ellie reached over and helped him. *CLICK.*

"Thanks," Grant said, sounding a little tense.

"You good?" Ellie asked.

"Yeah, I'm good," Grant claimed. "It's fine."

After a few minutes of waiting, they felt the plane take off and rise into the sky, headed for Biosyn Valley.

Maisie exited the mountain cabin eating a piece of toast. She decided to toss another log on the campfire. As she grabbed a chunk from the wood pile at the edge of the forest, she heard a noise.

Something was moving through the trees.

On edge, Maisie reached for the ax stuck in a nearby stump. But then she saw a juvenile *Velociraptor* emerge from the woods and take a few cautious steps into the cleared ground around their cabin.

"Hey," Maisie said, greeting the small dinosaur.

The raptor cocked her head, listening, curious.

Maisie held out her hand, showing the raptor what remained of her toast. "You like toast? It's got marmalade on it. Don't know if raptors are into marmalade." She tossed the toast onto the snowy ground. The raptor sniffed it, then gobbled it up enthusiastically.

"Huh. I guess they are. Next time, maybe we'll try peanut butter—"

"Maisie, don't move," Owen warned.

SNAP. A twig broke. Something had stepped on it. Standing still, Maisie looked past the juvenile raptor and saw her mother, Blue, creeping out of the forest, hissing. Maisie slowly backed away. Moving just as slowly, Owen came forward, putting himself a little nearer to Blue, raising his hands just as he had back in the days when he was training raptors.

"Hey, girl," he said to Blue in a calm but authoritative voice. "Staying out of trouble?"

Blue snapped at him aggressively. Her daughter ducked behind her.

"That's why I've been seeing two sets of tracks all winter," Owen said. "She looks just like you."

Never taking her eyes off the raptors, Maisie asked, "How'd she have a baby? It's impossible."

"They made her in a lab," Owen reminded her. "You never know with that stuff. No offense."

"None taken," Maisie said. "She won't hurt us, right?"

"Sure, she will," Owen said, not reassuring Maisie one bit. "Just breathe. She'll think you're scared if you don't breathe."

"I am scared," Maisie said.

"Yeah, but they don't have to know it."

The juvenile raptor scampered off into the woods. Staring at Owen, Blue growled and took a few steps back to the edge of the forest. She picked up a dead fox from the snowy ground and ran after her daughter.

"Get inside," Owen told Maisie as he started to follow Blue and her daughter into the trees.

"I want to come with you," Maisie protested.

"Maisie, get inside," Owen ordered.

Reluctantly, Maisie went into the cabin. Owen bent down, brushing his hands over the raptors' three-clawed footprints in the snow. He looked up at the forest and headed into the trees, following the tracks.

Not too far off, Delacourt spied on them through a pair of dirty binoculars. He watched Maisie enter the cabin, then saw Owen dart into the woods. He barked into his phone, "We gotta move."

"No," a woman's voice said. "Wait for our signal."

Inside the cabin, Maisie kicked snow off her boots and threw her coat down, angry at being left behind. As she stormed into her bedroom, Claire came out of hers to see what all the stomping and crashing was about. "Whoa! Hey, what's going on?"

WHAM! Maisie slammed her door closed.

"Not cool, Maisie," Claire called through the door. "You want to get out here and pick your coat up?" No answer. "Are you ignoring me?"

The door opened. Maisie swept out, picked up her coat, and defiantly passed Claire on her way to the front door. "Thanks for everything, Claire," she said. "It's been real."

"What? No! Get back here now!" Claire said, starting after her.

"You can't keep me here!" Maisie shouted as she went out the door. "You're not my mother!"

Claire stopped, thrown. By the time she got outside, Maisie was already heading down the road on her bike.

From his spot in the woods, Delacourt was watching through his binoculars. "She's leaving the house," 'ng reported into his phone.

'kay," the woman's voice said. "Go for the raptor."

d¹he abandoned school bus, Blue dropped the tee¹n the snow. Her daughter took the fox in her net ⌐dragged it a few feet until . . . *WHOOSH!* A and k⌐er and the fox into the air! She struggled WHA⌐n the trap. Blue screeched. *SKREEEE!*

Delaco⌐ hit Blue with his pickup truck, knocking her off⌐edge and into a deep ravine. "Grab it!"

Delacourt shouted to Wyatt and another poacher. "Let's go!"

The two men threw the netted juvenile into the back of their truck. Wyatt jumped into the driver's seat and revved the engine. As they rumbled away through the snow, Delacourt whooped in triumph, thinking of all the money he would get for the animal. From the truck bed, the young raptor cried for her mother.

But Blue was stuck in the deep ravine. She tried to jump out, but the cliff walls were too high and steep. She screeched again. *SKREEARRK!*

Not far off, Owen recognized Blue's cry. He ran toward the sound, arriving just in time to see the truck drive off. He locked eyes with Delacourt, who stuck a gun out the front passenger window and fired at Owen. *BLAM! BLAM!* The bullets splintered trees and branches around Owen. He had no choice but to duck for cover.

CHAPTER SEVEN

Maisie soon reached the old railroad bridge—the one Claire and Owen had warned her not to go past. She rode across it and screeched to a stop, but not because she was having second thoughts. A tan car blocked the road.

A man and a woman got out of the car and walked toward Maisie. The woman, whose name was O'Hara, said, "Maisie, thank God you're okay."

"Who are you?" Maisie asked, immediately suspicious.

"We've been looking for you a long time," O'Hara said.

Maisie wheeled around and started to go back the other way, but Delacourt's truck was already blocking the other end of the bridge.

Owen ran through the woods, heading toward the road, hoping to cut off the truck before it got away. But when he reached a high ridge, he looked down and saw Maisie being driven off in the back seat of the tan car. "NO!" he shouted.

As the tan car drove away, Delacourt's truck pulled up. He hopped out, picked up Maisie's bike, and threw it in the river. Then he got back in the truck and peeled out. Owen watched the truck go, his eyes burning with rage.

He rushed back to the cabin. Bursting through the door, he called out, "Claire!"

Claire came out of the bedroom. "She just took off again. I couldn't stop her."

"They found us," Owen said, storming over to a cabinet. "That rustler must have followed me here." He unlocked the cabinet and pulled out his rifle.

Claire's eyes widened in fear. "Where is she?"

"Get the truck," Owen answered.

Outside, Claire started to run toward their truck, but stopped in her tracks. Blue was stepping out of the snowy trees, her claws out and her teeth bared.

Owen stepped in front of Claire to protect her. "No," he barked at Blue. "NO!"

Blue lifted her head to the sky and screeched. *SKREEE!* Owen knew exactly why Blue was so mad. He'd spotted her daughter in the back of Delacourt's truck. "They took her kid, too," Owen told Claire. Then he looked Blue in the eye. "We're going to get her back, okay? I promise."

As Claire edged toward the truck, Owen stayed between her and Blue, keeping his hands up. "We're going to bring them both back."

With a lightning-fast move, Blue slashed Owen's open palm. Not deep —just a warning. Still, blood dripped onto the snow. Owen clenched his fist and extended his other hand to reassure Blue. With one last scream, she turned and disappeared into the woods. *SKREEEE!*

Owen and Claire raced down the mountain road, desperate to find Maisie. "There was someone else on the bridge," Owen said. "A woman. I've never seen her before. Those guys took a *Parasaurolophus* herd off me a few weeks back. Anything they steal leaves the mainland pretty quick. We don't have much time."

"Okay," Claire said, trying to reassure herself. "Maisie's smart. She can defend herself. We just have to stay calm."

"I'm going to rip that guy in half," Owen said, his jaw clenched.

"We can't go to the police," Claire said, thinking. "I know who to call."

At the offices of the Central Intelligence Agency's Dangerous Species Unit in San Francisco, Franklin was talking to a coworker about the locusts destroying fields in Nebraska, when his phone rang. It was an unknown number. He answered it anyway. "Hello?"

"Franklin," Claire said on the other end of the line.

Recognizing her voice immediately, he stepped around a corner and lowered his voice. "Okay, you're kind of a person of interest around this office, so I can't really be talking to—"

"I'm in trouble," Claire said, interrupting him. "I need your help."

"I could lose my job," Franklin protested. "And you know I'm not really qualified to do anything else, so—"

"We're outside," Claire said.

Franklin peeked through the blinds of a window and saw Claire and Owen looking up from the plaza below. "Okay, don't make eye contact with anyone," he instructed. "I'll meet you in the outdoor café. And get me a salted caramel brownie—those go fast."

Moments later, Owen, Claire, and Franklin were seated at a small table. Owen's injured hand was wrapped in a bandanna. Franklin brought up a secure CIA server on his tablet, clicked through a few screens, and showed a mug shot to Owen. "That him?"

It was Delacourt. "That's him," Owen replied.

"His name's Rainn Delacourt," Franklin said. "Real piece of work. What did he take?"

Owen and Claire exchanged a glance, hesitant to tell Franklin about Maisie being kidnapped. "Something we care about," Claire said. "Very much."

Franklin figured it out instantly. He lowered his voice. "I told you somebody would come looking for her. Claire, you can't just take a person."

CHAPTER EIGHT

"**W**e had no choice," Claire said firmly.

"Not in the eyes of the law," Franklin countered.

"Delacourt's not the law," Owen said. He pushed the salted caramel brownie across the table. "Here's your snack. Tell us where to find him."

Franklin picked up the brownie and took a bite. "Okay, if I even knew that," he said, chewing, "if I told you? Decades in jail."

Owen grabbed for his tablet, but Franklin held on to it. "Let it go. Let it go," he said as they struggled over the computer. Finally, Owen let go. They fell silent as a waiter arrived to pour more water in Franklin's glass.

"Thanks," Franklin said to the waiter. When he was gone, Franklin said, "Look, as far as we know, these guys only move dinosaurs. You really think they kidnapped Maisie?"

Owen and Claire looked desperate. Franklin began

typing on his tablet, swiping through pages. "We've been tracking him for a while," he said.

"So why's he still alive?" Owen asked.

Franklin looked up from his tablet in disbelief. "We can't just shoot him. We're tracking him to his buyer."

"Okay," Owen said. "Who's the buyer?"

Nervously eyeing a couple of guys in suits at a nearby table, Franklin asked, "Where did you call me from?"

Claire set a phone on the table. "It's a burner," she said, meaning it was a cheap disposable phone with prepaid minutes. Franklin picked it up and removed its battery.

"We don't know who Delacourt's buyer is . . . yet," Franklin said, looking over his shoulder to see if anyone was listening. "We've got a man on the inside. He's been with Delacourt for a couple of months." He showed them a picture of a man in a suit and tie. It was Wyatt, the guy who had warned Owen that Delacourt meant it when he said he'd kill him.

"I want to talk to him," Owen said.

"He's deep cover, man," Franklin protested. "We can't just call him."

"When did he last report in?" Claire asked, trying to be patient.

Franklin checked his tablet. "This morning. There's an exchange in Malta sometime tomorrow. Cash for cargo."

"Is Maisie with them?" Owen asked.

"No mention," Franklin said, shaking his head. "We have people on the ground in Malta already. One of them you know." On his tablet, he brought up a photo of Barry Sembené. He'd helped Owen train raptors at Jurassic World before the Indominus rex disaster. "Barry's French Intelligence now. Meet with him. Once we arrest Delacourt, we'll see if he knows where Maisie is. Our guys. Not you. Promise me you will not go in there and mess everything up."

"Nope," Owen said. "Wouldn't do that."

Franklin gulped water. "Look, you're both crazy. But you seem like you're good parents or whatever you're trying to be. She's lucky to have you. Don't get killed, okay?"

In northeastern Italy, the cargo plane carrying Drs. Grant and Sattler landed on a modern airstrip surrounded by the snowcapped Dolomite Mountains. An earnest young man named Ramsay Cole ran across the tarmac to enthusiastically welcome them to Biosyn Genetics.

"Dr. Sattler! Dr. Grant!" he said, shaking hands.

"I'm Ramsay Cole from Biosyn's Communications department. Everyone's so excited to have you. You're like legends around here."

"I think you have us confused with someone else," Sattler quipped.

"See? And so down-to-earth," Ramsay said. "I love that." He walked them through heavy wind to a sleek helicopter. "Amazing you're still so tight with Dr. Malcolm. You know how sometimes you meet your heroes and they disappoint you? He's exactly the way you want him to be."

"How much time have you spent with him?" Alan asked.

Ramsay grinned. "I know that was sarcastic, but honestly? Not enough. Watch your head." He ducked to avoid the helicopter's spinning propeller.

Alan looked at the chopper, hesitating. "This thing safe?"

"Don't worry," Ramsay assured him. "This one's a smooth ride."

They climbed in, and the helicopter flew over the mountains and descended into a deep valley of old-growth temperate rainforest. Ellie and Alan peered down as the chopper flew low over it.

"Biosyn bought this land for the amber deposits back in the nineties," Ramsay told them. "In the past few years, we've given sanctuary to over twenty displaced species—"

"Aren't we, uh, a bit low?" Alan said, sounding concerned.

"Restricted airspace," Ramsay replied. "Protects airborne life."

Alan looked up, nervously checking the skies for winged reptiles. He certainly didn't want to collide with one. Or with anything else.

"The first generation of dinosaurs came from Isla Sorna, but most of the Isla Nublar dinosaurs—from the original Jurassic Park—are here, too. It took the Department of Fish and Wildlife three years to catch the *T. rex,*" Ramsay said.

"She's here?" Grant asked tensely. Sattler didn't look thrilled at this news, either, given their experience with the *T. rex.*

"Arrived just before you did," Ramsay affirmed. "And of course the lab makes new ones for research."

On the ground below, a gigantic dinosaur lifted its head on its long neck. "Is that . . . *Dreadnoughtus?*" Alan asked, amazed.

"Beautiful, right?" Ramsay said, smiling. "Her name means 'fear nothing.' I've always loved that."

Alan smiled at his youthful enthusiasm.

"What do they graze on?" Ellie asked, always

curious about the connections between dinosaurs and plants.

"Hawthorn and fern," Ramsay answered. "All native to this area. Nothing is stocked except the deer population, which is a good species to support the top predator."

Grant raised an eyebrow as if to say, "And who would that be?"

Ramsay understood. "*Giganotosaurus*. At least for now."

Right on cue, a *Giganotosaurus* in the forest below roared as the helicopter buzzed overhead.

ROWWRRRR!

CHAPTER NINE

As they flew over an observation outpost above the trees, Dr. Sattler asked, "You never let people in the sanctuary with the dinosaurs, right?"

"Our research outposts are all connected underground," Ramsay explained. "No human feet touch the valley floor."

"Ever?" Alan asked skeptically. "What if an animal needs help?"

"We can herd the animals remotely," Ramsay answered. "Each one has a neural implant that sends electrical signals directly to the brain."

Alan frowned. "Doesn't that strike you as a bit—"

"Cruel?" Ellie said.

Ramsay shook his head. "It's actually super humane. You know how much voltage was in the old electric fences at Jurassic Park?"

"Yes," Alan said flatly. He remembered . . . vividly.

"This is like a fraction of that. The whole system

is next-level," Ramsay said proudly. "A breach in even one of our security barriers would require three unrelated systems to collapse. Independently."

Ellie and Alan exchanged an unconvinced glance. They'd heard talk like this before. *Our systems ensure nothing will go wrong.* And then things went terribly wrong.

"Uh-huh," Alan said.

The chopper landed on a helipad on top of Biosyn's research compound, a massive complex built underground. Trees on the roof made the facility invisible from above.

Ramsay led Ellie and Alan into the compound's central courtyard, which was buzzing with scientists and engineers. "Everyone's so young," Alan observed.

"Oh, we've attracted emerging talent from around the world," Ramsay said.

Lewis Dodgson, the head of Biosyn, crossed the courtyard to meet them, smiling broadly. "I can't believe it," he said. "Dr. Sattler. Dr. Grant. Here. Wow. I'm Lewis—"

"Dodgson," Ellie said, shaking his hand. "I didn't realize you'd be here."

"You're going to see some remarkable things today," he told them. "We are unlocking the true power of the genome. We're this close." He held his index finger and thumb about half an inch apart.

"Sounds lucrative," Ellie said.

A tiny frown flashed on Dodgson's face. "This isn't about money. We've identified dozens of applications for paleo-DNA. Cancer. Alzheimer's. We will be saving lives." His broad smile returned. "Wish I could show you around myself, but you're in capable hands with Ramsay." He clapped Ramsay on the shoulder. "We booked a private pod for your trip out. It'll take you through the caverns—you'll love it." He turned to Ramsay. "Better hurry. Malcolm's already speaking."

They reached a security checkpoint, where they had to surrender their phones. Sattler's was up-to-date, but Grant's was an old flip phone. Ramsay couldn't help but smile at the sight of it.

In a large hall, young Biosyn Genetics employees eagerly listened to Ian Malcolm's lecture on the dangers of unforeseen consequences. When he finished, they applauded enthusiastically.

Ellie and Alan approached him and asked to speak privately. As Ian led the way to a coffee stand in a large atrium, Ellie got right to the point. "Locusts," she said. "Altered with Cretaceous-era DNA. Designed to eat everything that isn't Biosyn seed."

"Mmm," Ian said, stepping briskly down a curved staircase. "Not my field."

"If these things continue to multiply," Ellie said, "we're looking at cascading system-wide effects."

"Gosh, that's awful," Ian replied lightly.

"What is the matter with you?" Alan asked sharply.

"I'm sorry, was there something you expected me to do?" Ian asked innocently. As they reached the coffee stand, he quickly glanced at the closed-circuit camera overhead and a nearby security guard. "Can I interest either of you in a cappuccino?" He addressed the guy behind the counter familiarly. "Tyler, two cappuccinos, please." Tyler picked up two cups.

"I don't want a cappuccino," Alan said.

"I can do a cortado if you'd rather have that," Tyler said, offering an alternative coffee drink.

"You need one," Ian assured Alan. "Trust me. The jet lag—it's really gotten to you."

"Oak milk or almond milk?" Tyler asked Alan.

"Do I look like I drink almond milk?" Alan asked testily.

Ellie caught the look on Ian's face and realized he was ordering cappuccinos for a reason. "Take the coffee, Alan," she said firmly.

CHAPTER TEN

When Tyler turned on the loud cappuccino machine, Ian dropped his voice so the security guard and the camera couldn't pick up what he was saying. "The locusts are part of a larger project called Hexapod Allies. You're exactly right about the intent."

He paused as Tyler turned off the machine, only resuming when the barista moved on to the second cappuccino. "I started hearing rumors six weeks ago. Then I read your piece on pesticides and put two and two together."

Alan was amazed by Ian's sudden change of tone and manner. But Ellie jumped right in. "The locusts are proliferating wildly. Living three, four times longer than they should. All my models show potential for a global ecological collapse."

Ian nodded slowly. "Locusts eat the crops. Humans go extinct. Dinosaurs inherit the earth." He leaned closer. "Downstairs. Sublevel six. Look for a lab marked L FOUR."

"We don't have access to sublevel—"

"Is that bamboo?" Ian asked, touching her shirt. "Sustainable. Look at this pattern. And so many pockets." He gripped her shoulder. "Seeing you is just wonderful." He turned to Alan. "Doctor." Then he abruptly walked away.

Ellie reached into her pocket and found an access band.

"What just happened?" Alan asked, bewildered.

"We're in," Ellie whispered.

But from the top of the staircase they had just descended, Lewis Dodgson watched suspiciously as Ellie and Grant rejoined Ramsay and continued on their tour of the complex.

Dodgson made his way down to sublevel six, gaining access with a band like the one Ian had slipped into Ellie's pocket. He walked determinedly up the hall to an advanced molecular genetics lab run by Dr. Henry Wu, the geneticist responsible for the first dinosaurs created at Jurassic Park.

Soon Dodgson and Wu were in a heated argument. "You don't understand," Wu told him. "The main locust blooms have moved into reproductive synchrony. This could cause global famine."

"We can't anticipate everything," Dodgson countered. "We'll tweak it."

Wu shook his head. "Their mass is growing exponentially. A week from now the swarm will cover six million square miles—"

"Henry," Dodgson said, cutting him off. "Let's not be afraid of our own success."

But Wu wasn't backing down. "We need to eradicate the ones we released. All of them."

"We don't want extinction," Dodgson insisted. "We want control."

"There is no such thing," Wu said. He shook his head. His experiences with Jurassic Park and Jurassic World had sunken in over the years.

Dodgson decided to play his trump card. "We found the girl."

Wu looked surprised. "You found her?"

"And the little raptor," Dodgson added. "Blue reproduced on her own, just like you said. I'll let you know when they arrive. Everything involving the girl goes through me, okay?"

"Is she all right?" Wu asked, looking concerned.

"She'd better be. She's the most valuable intellectual property on the planet." With that, Dodgson left the lab.

Maisie looked out the window of the private jet as it landed on a dirt runway. She didn't know it, but they were on Malta, an island in the middle of the Mediterranean Sea.

"Where are we?" Maisie asked.

The woman named O'Hara didn't answer.

"You said we were going somewhere safe," Maisie said accusingly. This isolated cargo airfield didn't look all that safe to her.

"You are," O'Hara said.

Through the window, Maisie spotted a woman in white standing on the tarmac next to two expensive black cars. Armed men stood on either side of her.

Maisie turned back to O'Hara. "You don't work for the government." In response, the woman gave the girl a look of faint pity.

Stairs lowered from the jet to the tarmac. As she descended, Maisie saw a small box with breathing holes being loaded into one of the black vehicles. It had arrived in a junky old military cargo plane known as a Fairchild C-119 Flying Boxcar.

Soyona Santos, the woman dressed in white, was staring at Maisie through dark sunglasses.

"Walk to the car," O'Hara ordered.

"No," Maisie said.

"It's not a choice," O'Hara said.

Realizing she had been thrust into a very danger-ous world, Maisie said, "I'll run."

"Go ahead, honey," O'Hara replied, daring her.

Maisie looked at the men holding guns and realized that this definitely wasn't her moment to escape. But she'd be watching for the right moment. . . .

As Maisie walked across the tarmac to Soyona Santos and the black car, she locked eyes with the pilot of the Fairchild C-119, who was being paid for flying Blue's daughter to Malta. The pilot was Kayla Watts, a former Air Force flier in her late twenties.

"What's with the girl?" Kayla asked, nodding toward Maisie.

"Not your problem," the man counting money said. The two black vehicles drove off with Maisie in one of them. The vehicles kicked up dust as they sped away. Kayla took the money from the guy.

"Good doing business," she said.

Owen and Claire made their way through the bus-tling streets of Valletta, the capital of Malta. Spotting them, Barry Sembené called, "Owen!"

The two friends reached each other and hugged.

"You finally got in shape," Barry teased. "I'm proud of you." He turned to Claire. "Hi, Claire," he said, giving her a friendly hug, too.

"I thought you'd end up in a quieter line of work," Claire said. "Not French intelligence."

"I tried," Barry said, shrugging. "My cousin and I opened a café, but I only lasted three weeks. The way the world is headed makes it hard to look away."

Barry led them through the crowded streets of the ancient city. "Dinosaurs are big business now," he said. "Europe, Middle East, Northern Africa—the trade all flows through Malta."

"You ever run into these guys before?" Owen asked, eager to get his hands on Maisie's kidnappers.

"Delacourt?" Barry said. He shook his head. "Until now he's been an American problem. We don't have intel on his cargo. Once they make the exchange, we'll see what they know about your girl."

Walking near the docks, they passed old fishing boats bobbing in the waves. "This place isn't too friendly to outsiders," Barry warned. "Don't look at anyone. Don't talk to anyone."

Past the docks, they reached an old building with a closed wooden door. Barry handed each of them a small earpiece and put one in his own ear. Owen and Claire did the same. "I told the team you'd listen in.

And that you won't interfere in any way. Which you will not, correct?"

"Absolutely not," Owen said.

"Noooo," Claire said.

Barry didn't believe them for a second. "Yeah, sure."

He dropped a coin into a cup held by an old man squatting near the door. The old man looked at Barry, took a flip phone out of his pocket, and typed a code. Barry opened the door, and they went down well-worn stone steps to a dark hallway.

CHAPTER ELEVEN

The hallway led to a vast underground market teeming with sellers and buyers. As Owen and Claire followed Barry past the stalls and booths, they were amazed and appalled by all the animals for sale.

An old woman was selling *Dimorphodons*—small winged reptiles—that were perched like birds in stacked cages.

A heavily tattooed man held a juvenile *Carnotaurus* on a chain. The man was missing a hand—probably bitten off by the *Carnotaurus*. As Owen walked by, the dinosaur snapped at him.

An open kennel with straw on the floor housed several *Microceratus*—small dinosaurs with mouths like beaks and frills at the back of their skulls.

A vendor called out in a language Owen and Claire didn't know, urging customers to buy handbags made from dinosaur hide. Claire winced at the sight of them, but Barry assured her, "It's okay—those are fake."

They passed a sizzling grill covered in dinosaur drumsticks the size of turkey legs. "But those aren't," Barry said.

A vendor offered a sample to Claire. "I'm good," she said.

"That legal?" Owen asked.

"There's no such thing as legal here," Barry said. *HISS!*

"Gah!" Claire exclaimed, startled by a foot-long hissing locust. A cage was full of the insects, crawling all over each other. Nearby, several were cooking on a grill.

"I know," Barry said, acknowledging the creepiness of the gigantic locusts. "They're everywhere now."

They passed Kayla Watts, the cargo pilot, sitting on a wooden crate. She glanced at the trio as they went by.

A gray-bearded man named Wigi approached Kayla. "You flying again today?"

"What's it to you?" Kayla asked.

"I've got cargo," Wigi said, nodding toward a crate. He started peeling bills off a thick roll.

"Don't tell me what it is," Kayla said. "Better I don't know."

"Elmisaurus," he said, naming a kind of toothless dinosaur that walked on its back legs. Wigi noted a dinosaur in a crate next to Kayla. *"Lystrosaurus?*

Very rare. I'll give you two thousand."

"Eight," Kayla countered. "He may be ugly, but he's got spirit."

Wigi slapped down a brick of bills. Kayla noticed a group of seedy characters whooping and hollering nearby. "You're going to put him in a fight?"

"He's mine now." Wigi smirked. "What do you care?"

Kayla looked into the *Lystrosaurus*'s eyes. For a moment, she felt torn. But finally, she said, "You'll be fine."

Moments later, in a fight ring, an *Oviraptor* puffed out its chest. The squat little *Lystrosaurus* stared at it, motionless. Spectators placed their bets.

When the *Oviraptor* struck at the *Lystrosaurus,* the smaller creature just chomped it, ending the fight with a single bite. Watching from a distance, Kayla smiled.

But then a fight broke out. Wigi pointed toward Kayla, and the *Oviraptor*'s owner rolled up his sleeves and headed her way, furious. Kayla stood up. "Is this what we're doing?" she sighed. "Okay, I got time."

Just a couple of minutes later, Claire was washing her hands in a dingy bathroom. Kayla walked in through the hanging beads that stood in for a door and started washing her hands, too. Blood ran down the drain. Claire noticed, and the two women's eyes met in the mirror.

"Chill," Kayla said. "It's not mine." She'd won her fight with the angry owner of the *Oviraptor*.

"You're American," Claire observed.

"That makes us friends?" Kayla asked. She dried her hands and left. Claire followed her back into the market.

"Wait," Claire said. "I'm looking for someone." She held up a photo of Maisie.

"Not interested," Kayla responded.

"She's all alone," Claire said.

Exhaling in frustration, Kayla took a look at the photo. Her expression changed. She recognized the girl she'd seen at the airstrip an hour ago. "This your daughter?" she asked.

"Yes," Claire said, keeping it simple.

"Sorry," Kayla said. "Can't get involved." She disappeared into the market. But once she'd gotten away, she looked back over her shoulder at Claire, concerned.

Later that day, acting on a tip, Barry, Owen, and Claire kept watch on the waterfront. Through a pair of binoculars, Owen spotted Delacourt and Wyatt stepping off a boat. "Here we go," Owen said.

"Target on the move," Barry said into a microphone.

In the waterfront café, a pair of undercover agents put down their newspapers and started following Delacourt and Wyatt.

Speaking into a radio, Owen said, "Claire, that's the guy. Long coat."

"I'm on him," Claire said through the radio.

Delacourt and Wyatt headed straight to the underground market, weaving between the stalls. Barry and Owen followed, keeping a safe distance behind. Claire tracked Delacourt from the next aisle over.

Soyona Santos walked up to Delacourt and Wyatt.

"Who's that?" Owen hissed to Barry.

"Soyona Santos," Barry said, keeping his voice low. "She's a broker for people who don't want to be seen."

"My people say the raptor arrived in good condition," Santos said, sounding surprised that Delacourt had managed to do something right.

"Catching a thing ain't easier 'cause it's small," Delacourt said. "Never been happier to drop a piece of cargo. She's a pistol."

Claire caught Owen's eye. Were they talking about Maisie?

"I have another job for you," Santos said. "Short hop. Money's double."

"What's the cargo?" Delacourt asked.

One of Santos's men flipped the canvas cover off a truck, revealing four reinforced iron boxes with tiny air holes. Inside the nearest box, an animal growled. Delacourt tensed up.

"Fifty thousand to fly them to Riyadh," Santos said.

"Seventy-five," Delacourt countered.

"Done," Santos replied.

"All right," Delacourt said, smiling. "Load 'em up."

Santos nodded to one of her men, who brought out a small bag of cash. An undercover agent stationed nearby took photos through a long lens of the money changing hands. "Confirmed," he said into his radio.

Like a wave, agents swept in, shouting. Snipers popped up and took aim.

CHAPTER TWELVE

Wyatt, though working undercover, pulled out a gun and pointed it at Delacourt. "Don't move!" he yelled. "Hands in the air!"

A gunfight broke out between the CIA agents and Santos's guards. In the confusion, Delacourt ran off. The truck with the four iron boxes peeled out. Santos slipped through an open door.

Owen went after Delacourt, and Claire followed Santos.

Chained dinosaurs squawked and screeched as Delacourt and Owen ran through the dense maze of stalls. When he caught up with Delacourt, Owen tackled the poacher into a stack of wooden cages. Shrieking and fluttering their wings, tiny *Dimorphodons* escaped from the broken cages, hopping away.

Facing off against Owen, Delacourt pulled out a knife. Owen drew his knife, too, but Delacourt managed to stab him in the leg. Grimacing, Owen stumbled,

Dimorphodons flapping their clipped wings around him.

BLAM! Delacourt shot a rusty ring off a wall, releasing two chained-up dinosaurs—a *Baryonyx* and a *Carnotaurus.* They lurched forward, whipping their chains and roaring. *ROWWRR!*

Delacourt tried to exit the underground market, but Owen tackled him into the fight ring where the *Lystrosaurus* had bested the *Oviraptor.* "The girl," Owen barked. "Where did you take her?" Instead of answering, Delacourt kicked Owen's hand with his boot, sending his knife clattering away.

Delacourt lunged with his knife, but Owen managed to grab his wrist. As they struggled, the *Lystrosaurus* bit Delacourt's leg and wouldn't let go.

"Get it off!" Delacourt screamed.

"Where is she?" Owen asked.

"We handed her off to Santos," Delacourt replied, trying to shake off the *Lystrosaurus.* "Both of 'em. I don't know where she took 'em after that!"

RIP! Delacourt's pants leg tore, freeing him from the dinosaur's bite. He started to run off, but the *Baryonyx* got to him before he could escape. *CHOMP!*

Looking away from the carnage, Owen spoke into his radio. "Claire! Are you still following Santos?"

"I got her," Claire replied, tracking the woman in white through the crowds on the streets of Valletta.

Barry and the other CIA agents had laid down a spiked strip to stop the truck. With its tires shredded, it swerved and crashed into a stone wall. The four iron boxes slid off the back of the truck onto the cobblestones. As Barry and the agents approached, the truck's driver pressed a button on a remote. *CLANK!* The iron boxes opened . . . and four *Atrociraptors* leapt out, sniffing the air and baring their teeth. They were fast, strong . . . and trained to kill.

Santos used a laser pointer to identify targets, then pressed a button on a device that emitted a high-pitched sound, signaling for one of the *Atrociraptors* to attack. She targeted Barry and two agents.

Barry dove into a fishing boat, hotly pursued by the *Atrociraptor.*

Santos ran into an old apartment building and entered an apartment with a window where she could see what was happening below. Claire followed, confronting Santos in a kitchen. "Okay, listen—" Claire said.

Santos snatched a paring knife off the counter and lunged with it. Claire had come prepared. She whipped out a shock stick that was used by smugglers to control dinosaurs. Defending herself, she used it on Santos. *ZZZT!*

"Nnnghh!" Santos groaned as she crumbled to the floor. "You don't use it on *people*."

"Where's my daughter?" Claire demanded.

"She wasn't yours to keep," Santos said.

"Where is she? Tell me!" Claire said, threatening another shock.

"Biosyn!" Santos blurted. "They took her to Biosyn."

ROWRR! One of the *Atrociraptors* smashed through the door! As it landed in front of Claire, she shocked it. It recoiled. Santos aimed a red dot of laser light at Claire's neck, targeting her.

Claire dove into a bedroom and slammed the door. *CRASH!* The *Atrociraptor* splintered the wood of the old door. As it broke through, Claire jumped out an open window onto a roof below.

But the predator kept on coming, chasing Claire across rooftops and down a stone stairwell.

CHAPTER THIRTEEN

Working together, Owen and Barry managed to lure one of the *Atrociraptors* back into its iron box and slam the door closed. But Claire was still running from the other *Atrociraptor,* trying to lose it in another apartment.

It kept coming, relentlessly.

Claire jumped off a balcony and caught the guard-rail of a lower balcony just as the *Atrociraptor* smashed through the window above her. *TRSHSSH!*

Hearing the glass shatter, Kayla looked up from the street below. When she saw Claire dangling, she knew she had to help her.

Claire fell, breaking through the canvas roof of a three-wheeled minitruck. Kayla jumped in behind the wheel and said, "Hang on tight."

VRRRIM! She hit the gas, and they took off, the *Atrociraptor* racing after them. They dodged obstacles as the fierce beast lunged and snapped at them.

"Why are you helping me?" Claire asked, astonished.

"'Cause you need help," Kayla answered simply.

"I told you I needed help!" Claire said. Then she radioed Owen, "I know where Maisie is! There's an airfield on the north side of the island. Meet us there."

Just as he got Claire's message, Owen saw Barry and Wyatt spin toward him with their weapons drawn. "Whoa!" he cried, holding up his hands. "Hey, fellas!"

But they weren't aiming at Owen. Soyona Santos was just behind him. "Get down on the ground!" Barry ordered. He nodded at Owen and said, "Go," having heard Claire's message.

As Owen sped off on a motorcycle, Santos used her laser pointer to mark him as a target—twice. Two *Atrociraptors* blasted out of a dark alley in vicious pursuit.

In the three-wheeled minitruck, Claire tried to bash the *Atrociraptor* with a tire iron, but the dinosaur snatched it in its jaws and tossed it aside. Claire picked up a long steel bar, thinking of throwing it like a javelin, but as they approached a narrow alley, she saw an opportunity. She turned the bar horizontal. It caught on the stone walls, clotheslining the raptor. *WHACK!*

On the motorcycle, Owen tore through high-speed traffic, weaving and dodging, trying to shake the two

68

Atrociraptors. They stayed right with him.

The minitruck sped onto the airfield where the old Fairchild C-119 Flying Boxcar was parked. Kayla jumped out, climbed into her plane, and fired up the propellers. Claire hurried into the cargo plane, too. Through the window, she saw Owen roar up on the motorcycle.

"Open up the back!" she shouted.

"You know this guy?" Kayla asked.

Gaining speed on the runway, the plane opened its back doors and a ramp lowered. Owen zoomed up the ramp and crashed into the cargo hold. The plane rose into the air, leaving the *Atrociraptors* behind.

Claire and Owen pushed through a beaded curtain into the cockpit. Claire quickly strapped herself into the copilot's seat.

"Kayla Watts," Kayla said, introducing herself to Owen. "You're welcome."

"You two know each other?" Owen asked, confused.

"We met in the ladies' room," Kayla explained. "I'll take you to Biosyn, but I can't promise it won't be dangerous."

"You don't look like you fly for Biosyn," Owen said.

"I fly for whoever pays me," Kayla said, "but we'll call this one a favor."

"You'd risk your life for a kid you never met?" Owen asked.

Kayla shrugged. "You wanna ask questions, or you want a ride?"

Claire and Owen looked at each other. What choice did they have?

"We'll take the ride," Owen said.

"Strap in," Kayla ordered. "And when we get there, let me do the talking. They don't exactly like unexpected guests."

As Ramsay wrapped up Ellie and Alan's tour of Biosyn, Ellie asked, "Do you create new species here?"

"Nah," Ramsay said, shaking his head, "we don't do that here. I like to think we've evolved. Look, we still have some time before your pod ride. You guys want to look around?"

Dr. Sattler saw an opportunity to get down to the lab Ian had mentioned. "Uh, sure. Yeah."

"Okay," Ramsay said, smiling. "I'll meet you at the hyperloop. Station three. The elevator's down the hall."

Alan and Ellie waited until Ramsay was out of sight, then headed toward the elevators to the restricted levels. They spotted workers peeling off white coveralls and tossing them into bins to be sterilized.

Ellie got an idea. . . .

Moments later, dressed in slightly wrinkled lab coveralls, Ellie and Alan entered one of the elevators. "Please try to blend in," Ellie said.

"I am trying," Alan protested. He held the access band to the elevator's panel. *BEEP.* It flashed green. Taking a deep breath, he pressed the bottom button for sublevel six. The doors closed.

In Henry Wu's lab, Blue's daughter banged her snout against the bars of her cage, furious at her imprisonment. Henry crouched in front of the cage. "I'm sorry it had to happen like this," he said.

"Yep, that's what kidnappers say," Maisie told him, angry and scared.

He stood and took a couple of steps toward her. "Claire should never have hidden you away. You're very important, Maisie. To the whole world."

Maisie looked at the young raptor. "You took her, too?"

"We needed her to help us understand you."

Bending down in front of the cage, Maisie said, "Hey, Beta. You okay?"

"Is that her name?" Henry asked.

"I gave it to her," Maisie said.

Henry smiled. "Well, Beta is very special. When we created Blue, we used monitor lizard DNA to fill gaps in her genome. Monitors can reproduce without a mate. That's why Blue has the ability to bear offspring all on her own."

SNAP! Beta bit the air, twitching with rage.

"Blue and Beta are genetically identical," Henry explained. "Like you and—"

"Charlotte," Maisie said.

"What do you know about her?"

Maisie sighed. "She died a long time ago. It broke my grandpa's heart, so he made me."

"Actually, Maisie, he didn't," Henry said. "Charlotte made you."

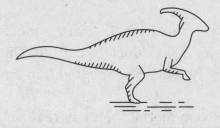

CHAPTER FOURTEEN

Henry Wu sat Maisie down at a table near Beta's cage and brought up video copied from a 1987 VHS tape on a computer monitor. Maisie saw a thirteen-year-old girl who looked exactly like her: Charlotte Lockwood. Behind her were incubators in a laboratory.

"Another one hatched today!" Charlotte said right into the camera, clearly excited. *"Microceratus.* She looked like a turtle without a shell."

The video cut to a scene of Charlotte rolling a rubber ball toward a colorful *Microceratus.* To the girl's delight, the little dinosaur rolled the ball back with its snout.

Speechless, Maisie watched the identical twin she'd never met.

"Charlotte grew up around scientists," Henry said. "Eventually she became one herself. She was brilliant in ways I'll never be." He changed the video to one of Charlotte in her thirties. She was clearly pregnant.

Maisie's eyes widened. "Is that . . . me?"

"Yes," Henry said. "Just like Blue, Charlotte had a child all by herself. She created you from her own DNA."

"So I do have a mother," Maisie realized.

"Your grandfather didn't want anyone to know. He had to protect her, and you."

"And we're the same?"

Henry frowned. "You were. But when Charlotte was older she got very sick with a genetic disorder. The symptoms didn't appear until after you were born." He clicked on another video.

"Good morning," Charlotte said into the camera. "This is day five of therapeutic gene delivery."

"Do I have it, too?" Maisie asked.

"No," Henry said. "Charlotte did the impossible. She changed your DNA. She altered every cell in your body to eradicate the disease."

"How?" Maisie asked.

"With a virus," Wu said. "No one on earth has ever known how to do that, to this day."

On the monitor, Maisie, only eighteen months old, climbed onto Charlotte's knee. "Can you say hi to the camera?" Charlotte asked her.

"She fixed me," Maisie said, watching herself. Charlotte gave her toddler a hug, then picked up a syringe and gave her a tiny injection.

"Charlotte's discovery is part of you now," Henry said. "Your DNA could change the world. I have to know how she did it. I have all her records, all her research, but I can't replicate her work. If I could study you and Beta—whose DNA was never changed—I could fix a terrible mistake."

Maisie looked alarmed. "What kind of mistake?"

After hesitating a moment, Henry pointed to a table. On it, one of the enormous engineered locusts was partially dissected. Maisie was horrified. But she was also fascinated. If this scientist understood how her mother had changed her DNA with a virus, could he actually fix these monster bugs?

"Little science class?" Lewis Dodgson walked into the lab and bent down to get on Maisie's level. "Maisie, I know this all feels strange, but we're going to do everything we can to make this place feel like home." He looked at Henry. "Got a second?" Dodgson led the way into a side office.

"I'll be right back," Henry said.

As they went into the office, Maisie heard Dodgson say, "What are you showing her? You have no right—"

Maisie had heard enough. She had to get out of there. And fast.

Ellie and Alan found a greenhouse full of buzzing locusts. They went in, and Ellie had Alan pick up one of the locusts so she could swab a DNA sample out of its mouth. She needed genetic proof that Biosyn was engineering locusts that would destroy non-Biosyn crops.

As Alan held it, the fluttering locust turned yellow. It brushed its legs against another locust, and that one turned yellow, too. As the locusts jostled and churned, more and more of them turned yellow, becoming increasingly agitated.

"That's not good," Alan said, alarmed.

Maisie bent down by Beta, who screeched. *SKREE!* "You want to get out of here?" Maisie asked the little raptor. "Me too." She picked up a metal stool and smashed the lock on the cage. The door swung open, and Beta burst free, crashing into a table of equipment.

Dodgson and Henry rushed back into the room. Beta leapt onto a counter and hissed at them.

While they were distracted, Maisie slipped into an area of industrial pipes leading to lower areas of the complex—an escape route. She started climbing down. Beta raced out of the lab.

Dodgson hit an alarm button on the wall.

Just as Ellie finished collecting the DNA sample, the alarm blared, sending the locusts into a frenzy.

"Go! GO!" Alan shouted.

WHOOOM!

The locusts rose into a swarm, filling the greenhouse with their vibrating wings. "Stay low!" Alan advised. He and Ellie crawled toward the door. They got through it with their access band, but a dozen giant locusts flew into the small decontamination chamber with them. Before Alan could open the second door, locusts knocked the access band out of his hand.

The swirl of locusts made it impossible to see. Alan groped along the floor for the band. Trapped in the small room, he and Ellie were getting battered by the spiky locusts.

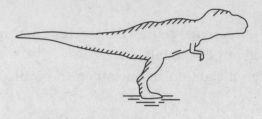

CHAPTER FIFTEEN

Maisie shinnied down the big pipe and dropped onto the floor. She picked a direction and ran down a hallway. The alarm was still blaring, and a voice came over a loudspeaker, announcing that an asset had escaped.

She reached a corner and stopped. Hearing a furious pounding, she walked toward the noise to see where it was coming from. In a small glass room, two people in white coveralls were lying on the floor, hitting the glass. Angry locusts swarmed around them.

Finally, Dr. Grant found the access band. He lifted it to the panel and opened the door. He and Ellie tumbled out into the hall, shutting the door behind them, trapping the locusts inside.

Except for one. Alan stomped on it. *SPLAT.*

Breathing hard, Dr. Sattler and Alan turned and saw Maisie looking them up and down. When they pulled off their headgear, she recognized them from pictures at her grandfather's house. "What are you doing here?" she asked.

"What are *you* doing here?" Ellie countered, surprised to see a young girl in this research facility.

Maisie looked at the buzzing insects in the chamber. She instantly guessed that Ellie and Alan had snuck into a place where they weren't supposed to be. Maybe these two people would help her escape. "I'm Maisie Lockwood," she told them.

Ellie looked at her, stunned. She knew that name well. "Oh," she said. "Look, we don't work for Biosyn. Actually, we've got to get out of here."

Maisie and Ellie locked eyes. "So do I," Maisie replied with a quick nod of complicity.

Ellie and Alan exchanged a look. Saving Maisie Lockwood was a responsibility they hadn't bargained for. But they didn't hesitate.

The three of them were going to escape Biosyn right now. Together.

Kayla steered her old Fairchild C-119 Flying Boxcar over snowcapped peaks, carrying Owen and Claire to Biosyn Genetics in Italy's Dolomite Mountains.

Heavy sheets of fog obscured the land below. "Okay," she said. "In and out. We find your girl and go. You ready?"

Claire and Owen nodded. Kayla picked up the radio's microphone and tried to sound as casual as possible. "Tower, this is N141. Request to land for freight delivery. Over."

A moment later, a female voice crackled over the speaker in response. "N141, negative. You are not cleared to land. Over."

Claire looked at Owen, worried. He tried to give her a reassuring look.

"Uh, copy that, tower," Kayla said, keeping her voice neutral. "Be advised shipment is perishable. Over."

"Negative, N141," the voice from the tower repeated. "We've been informed you're carrying unauthorized passengers. Return to point of origin. Over."

Kayla released the button on the mic and turned to her passengers. "Someone tipped them off. You two must be important."

She pressed the button, ready to try a new tactic.

In the control room at Biosyn, giant screens showed all areas of the research facility. About a dozen technicians were scattered around the large room. On one side, an air traffic controller studied the screens in front of her.

Kayla's voice came out of a speaker. "Tower, we have a sick passenger. We need immediate clearance. Over."

Lewis Dodgson stood over the air traffic controller's shoulder, glaring down at the speaker, thinking. The air traffic controller looked up at him. He shook his head no.

The air traffic controller spoke into her headset. "Negative. Return to point of origin. We will dispatch security measures."

Kayla pretended not to hear this. "Tower, are you guys hearing that static? I'm hearing, like, a low hum."

"Nice try, Kayla," the air traffic controller said. "They will down your bird."

"Who is this . . . Denise?" Kayla's voice said through the speaker. "Want me to start spilling secrets, Denise? Remember Dubrovnik?"

Denise looked up at Dodgson, horrified. He didn't look bothered at all. "She must mean a different Denise," she assured him.

On another bank of monitors, Dodgson saw flashing lights and guards prowling through halls looking for Beta. His head of security entered the control room, and the two of them stepped aside to speak privately.

"I talked to Santos," the security head reported. "It's the girl's parents. They followed her to Malta, and now they're flying here."

Dodgson thought for a moment, then said, "Shut down the Aerial Deterrent System."

The head of security raised his eyebrows. "You sure?"

Dodgson looked very sure. And he was not used to having his decisions questioned.

From the cockpit of her plane, Kayla steered through the thickening fog. Suddenly a metal box on the control panel blinked red and a buzzer sounded. *BZZZZZT-BZZZZZT-BZZZZZT.*

"What's that?" Owen asked, not liking the sound of what was clearly some kind of warning.

"Aerial Deterrent System," Kayla explained. "Keeps the airborne life away."

"Why's it blinking?" Claire asked.

"Because buzzkill Denise in the tower just turned it off!" Kayla snapped. "We gotta get out of this airspace."

In the fog above them, they spotted a silhouette. "That's another airplane, right?" Owen said. The silhouette flapped its wings. "Uh, not exactly," Kayla answered.

A flying pterosaur the size of a private jet emerged from the thick fog.

"What is that thing?" Claire asked.

"*Quetzalcoatlus,*" Kayla said. "Late Cretaceous. Should have stayed there."

The *Quetzalcoatlus* shrieked and disappeared

into the fog above. Silence. "Okay, cool," Kayla said, relieved. "It's gone."

FWOOM! The beast swooped down out of the mist, spreading its massive wings. It clamped its talons onto the World War II plane, ripping one of its wing engines off. *BOOM!* The engine exploded. Every alarm in the cockpit went off at once. *FWEE! FWEET! FWEEEET!*

The *Quetzalcoatlus* opened its talons, and the plane dropped twenty feet. Air roared through holes in the fuselage. Kayla, Owen, and Claire were tossed around violently.

"Fifteen thousand feet!" Kayla shouted. "If you're gonna eject, now's the time!" She eyed Owen. "I only have one ejection seat. You're in it."

"You don't have parachutes?" Owen asked incredulously.

"I wasn't expecting company!" Kayla yelled.

Acting quickly, Owen pulled Claire into the ejection seat. "Okay, listen to me. Claire, you've got to get off this plane."

"What?" Claire gasped.

"I said you gotta—"

"I HEARD WHAT YOU SAID!"

"The parachute will open by itself," he instructed her, trying to keep his voice calm. "If it doesn't, pull this red cord here. Got it?"

"Ten thousand feet!" Kayla shouted.

Owen put Claire's hand on the ejection lever next to her seat. "Look at me. You're the one who's going to get to Maisie. You're her shot. You're her mom."

Clenching her jaw, Claire nodded.

"I'll see you again," Owen said. "I promise." He kissed her, and Claire yanked the lever. *POOM!* The ejection seat fired, blasting her out of the cockpit.

Claire fell through the hard wind, the plane and the *Quetzalcoatlus* above her and Biosyn Valley below. *Pteranodons* swooped down, snapping their jaws around her.

WHOOM! She deployed her parachute. But a *Pteranodon* tore its fabric. She struggled, tumbling in the chair, plunging toward the valley floor. She smashed through the tree canopy. Branches cracked, barely breaking her landing.

CHAPTER SIXTEEN

Back in the plane, Owen strapped into the copilot seat of the descending aircraft. "What's the plan?"

"Whatever happens," Kayla answered, struggling with the controls, "that's the plan."

He looked out the cockpit window. *SPOOOSH!* The plane crashed into a frozen lake with an icy dam at one end.

In the Biosyn control room, an engineer studied a display. "Looks like they hit the dam."

Dodgson surveyed the big map of the valley. "Get a drone out there," he commanded. "If there are survivors, we need to find them before something else does."

Claire opened her eyes. She was bruised, but no bones were broken, as far as she could tell. Still strapped into the ejector seat, she hung from the branch of a tall tree, fifteen feet above the ground. Below, she saw a deer eating vegetation near a shallow, muddy pool.

Before she could unbuckle herself, Claire saw a twenty-foot-long dinosaur with feathers and long claws emerge from the woods. The *Therizinosaurus* passed by Claire, inches from her head, and struck the deer like lightning. But it didn't eat the carcass. It began to feed on the vegetation the deer had been eating. The herbivore was protecting its territory.

Claire slowly released herself from the harness and dropped to the ground. The *Therizinosaurus* heard her and turned, searching. Crawling across the ground, Claire reached the muddy pool and slipped in, submerging herself. The dinosaur hissed and left.

Above a ridge, Claire saw a plume of black smoke rising. From the plane crash? Had Owen survived?

Black smoke rose from the wrecked Fairchild C-119, half-submerged in the frozen lake. *CRACK!* As it slipped farther in, Owen and Kayla broke open a side hatch and climbed out onto the ice. Bruised and battered, Owen surveyed the wreckage. "I don't think they'll be able to salvage your plane."

"That was my baby," Kayla said softly.

She looked around. Near the shore of the lake, a blue light pulsed through the mist. It had to be a structure of some kind, serving Biosyn employees.

Owen spotted the light, too. "Okay," he said. "We're going to very carefully walk to shore."

Kayla agreed. They stood. The ice cracked but held. They started making their way across, taking slow steps.

"Where'd you learn to fly?" Owen asked, trying to keep things ordinary and relaxed.

"Air Force," Kayla said. "It's in my family. On my mother's side."

"Navy," Owen said, identifying the military branch his family had always joined.

"Clearly," Kayla said. The ice cracked near her feet. The two froze. Then they moved on.

"How'd you end up running freight for dinosaur dealers?" Owen asked.

"I was a legitimate contract pilot before, but it didn't pay enough," Kayla explained. "Honestly, though, I think I'm done with this line of work."

"Is that why you're helping us?"

"I was there when Santos handed your girl off

to Biosyn. I could have said something. I didn't," Kayla admitted. "And when I saw her picture . . ." She shook her head. "It isn't enough to do nothing."

"Thank you," Owen said, meaning it. The ice moved beneath Kayla's feet, and he grabbed her arm, steadying her.

On shore, an animal darted behind some rocks. "You see that?" Owen said. There was a flash of red. "Something's watching us." Owen unsheathed his knife, and Kayla drew a shock stick out of a holster.

Then they saw it. A *Pyroraptor*—a carnivorous dinosaur with feathers the color of fire.

"Don't look it in the eyes," Owen warned. "It'll read that as aggression—a challenge."

"What eyes?" Kayla asked. "I see teeth. Claws. Feathers. They've got feathers now?"

"Always did," Owen said.

Lowering its head, the *Pyroraptor* stepped out onto the ice, hunting its prey. Owen and Kayla backed away from it.

The plane slipped, opening a wide crack between them and the *Pyroraptor.* The dinosaur eyed the opening, dove in, and swam beneath the ice, hungrily looking up at the two humans. Owen and Kayla backed toward the dam as the ice cracked around them, until . . .

CRACK! SPLASH! The ice broke under Owen's feet, and he fell in! The *Pyroraptor* swam rapidly toward him, but Kayla yanked Owen out of the frigid water before the dinosaur could bite him.

ROWR! Denied its prey, the furious *Pyroraptor* rose out of the water. Not wanting to waste their momentary advantage, Owen and Kayla climbed onto the dam and ran toward the blue light at the end of a metal walkway on the edge of the lake. The *Pyroraptor* scrambled to its feet and shook the moisture from its feathers. Then it moved toward them with its claws bared.

Spotting a service elevator, Kayla and Owen dove and rolled into it. Owen slammed the metal grate shut just before the raptor pounced, tearing at them through the bars.

ZZTTZZZTCH! Kayla zapped the *Pyroraptor* with her shock stick. It screamed in pain. Owen slapped a button with his palm and the elevator rattled to life, descending. Kayla and Owen looked at each other.

"You good?" Owen asked.

"Yeah, yeah, not shook at all," Kayla lied. "You?"

"Nah," Owen claimed.

CHAPTER SEVENTEEN

Having disposed of their white coveralls, Ellie, Alan, and Maisie ran into the hyperloop station that Biosyn employees used to move gear around the valley. A pod built of glass and metal waited in the underground tube. Alan tried using the access band to power up the pod, but nothing happened.

"Great," he said, frustrated.

Hearing footsteps in the hallway, they spun around and saw Ramsay. Maisie ducked around a corner. Ellie tried to cover, speaking casually. "You know this place is a maze? I thought we were straight-up lost, but then Alan remembered you said station three—"

"Do you have it?" Ramsay asked urgently.

"What?" Alan asked, acting as though he had no idea what Ramsay was asking about. He turned to Ellie. "What is he talking about?"

"We were only taking the tour," Ellie said.

"The DNA sample," Ramsay responded. "Do you have it?"

Alan and Ellie were speechless. From the looks on their faces, Ramsay assumed they had the DNA sample they had come for. He fired up the hyperloop pod, punching in an override code written on his hand. "This pod will take you straight to the airfield. We have a plane ready to fly. Don't waste any time."

"Ian told you about the Hexapod Allies," Ellie said, referring to Biosyn's scheme to engineer the locusts and put all their seed competitors out of business.

"Nope," Ramsay said. "I told him."

Stunned, Ellie asked, "You did all of this from the inside?"

The door to the pod opened, and Ramsay ushered them in.

"Wait," Alan said.

Behind Ramsay, Maisie stepped out of hiding. Ramsay turned and was amazed to see her. "Maisie Lockwood," he said in surprise.

She nodded. Ramsay stepped aside, gesturing for her to get in the pod with Ellie and Alan. "Go," he said.

In the Biosyn control room, Dodgson's head of security showed him footage of Ellie and Alan entering the locust greenhouse. "How'd they get in there?" Dodgson asked angrily.

"They used an access key," the security head explained. "One of our cameras caught Ian Malcolm putting something in Sattler's pocket."

"I want to see him," Dodgson snarled. "Get Ramsay up here, too. Where are Sattler and Grant now?"

"They caught the hyperloop right on schedule," the security guy reported.

Dodgson got an idea.

The pod zipped through the tube. Dr. Sattler saw that Maisie was nervous. "You know, I knew your mom. She lectured at the university. We became friends."

"What was she like?" Maisie asked curiously.

"Brilliant. Light-years ahead of everyone."

"And I was her experiment."

"No," Ellie assured her. "She wanted a child more than anything. I didn't know her long, but I know she must have loved you very much."

BZZZZ! The pod slowed to a stop, and the lights flickered off. The pod's door swung open. Ellie got out

T. REX

NAME MEANS "TYRANT LIZARD"

The *Tyrannosaurus rex*—*T. rex*—is the ultimate apex predator, but now she has new carnivores to compete with, including the *Allosaurus*, *Baryonyx*, and equally fierce *Giganotosaurus*.

DINOSAUR INDEX

BLUE

VELOCIRAPTOR

SUB-FILE: BETA
CLONE

NAME MEANS "SWIFT THIEF"

Blue the *Velociraptor* has always been the leader of her pack. This time she is protecting her own clone—baby raptor Beta—and teaching her to survive.

DIMETRODON

NAME MEANS
"TWO MEASURES OF TEETH"

This reptile has a mouth full of cone-shaped teeth that she uses for grabbing slippery frogs and fish to eat. Her most distinguishing feature is the large fin on her back.

QUETZALCOATLUS

NAME MEANS "FEATHERED SERPENT"

Named after an Aztec feathered serpent god, she is the largest flying creature to ever take to the skies.

SAURUS

NAME MEANS "GIANT SOUTHERN LIZARD"

The *Giganotosaurus* is the largest-known carnivore to walk the earth—again! Now that this predator's back, no one and nothing is safe from this formidable threat.

PYRORAPTOR

NAME MEANS "FIRE THIEF"

From dense jungles to snowy mountains, the fiery-feathered hunter known as the *Pyroraptor* has spread out through many environments, always looking for the next meal.

and found an emergency box on the wall. She grabbed two flashlights and shined one down a long tunnel.

"These are the old amber mines," Alan said.

"I'll stay here," Maisie said from inside the pod.

"That's probably not all that reasonable," Alan argued.

"You want to go into the dark tunnel. I want to stay in the bulletproof tube. Who's unreasonable?" Maisie asked stubbornly.

"The bulletproof tube has its door stuck open," Alan pointed out. Then he softened his tone. "Listen, I know how you feel. But Dr. Sattler's a good person to have in a tight spot, and this is a tight spot. So come on, let's go."

Convinced, Maisie climbed out of the pod, and the three of them headed into the caves. In an underground lake behind them, a frilled fin rippled the water.

On a monitor, Dodgson read that the pod was STOPPED and POWERED DOWN in the amber mines. His head of security gave him a look that said "You sure about this?" Dodgson turned off the monitor so no one else could see that he had deliberately shut the pod down.

Ramsay entered. "Everything all right? I heard the alarm."

"Nothing we can't handle," Dodgson said. "You were with Grant and Sattler the whole time, right?"

Though he knew he was being accused of slipping up, Ramsay stayed cool. "I left them in the commissary for lunch. I had some business to handle. Maybe forty-five minutes? Otherwise, yeah, I stayed with them."

"And they made it out okay?" Dodgson asked.

"Yep," Ramsay said, nodding. "On the hyperloop now. Might be on the plane already."

Ian Malcolm walked in. "You called?"

"Dr. Malcolm, you're fired," Dodgson said, getting right to the point.

"What?" Ramsay said, shocked.

Malcolm sighed and muttered, "And it was such a cushy gig."

CHAPTER EIGHTEEN

An alarm flashed on the console. "One of the hyper-loop pods shut down in the amber mines," Denise reported.

Dodgson faked complete ignorance of the breakdown. "Wow. This day," he said in an exasperated voice. "Which one?"

"A-seven," Denise said. "Unresponsive. Kind of bizarre."

"Are there dinosaurs in the mines?" Ian asked.

"There are dinosaurs everywhere," an engineer said. "Birds are dinosaurs."

Staring at the graphic on the console, Ramsay looked concerned. "A-seven is Grant and Sattler's pod. We need to send a security team out there now."

Dodgson took a step toward him. "Ramsay, I've always appreciated that you stay in your lane. We'll take it from here."

Ian frowned. "That's it, huh? Nothing else to see here."

"I don't admire your tone," Dodgson said, turning toward him.

"I don't admire your willful genetic experimentation," Ian said, bringing the matter out into the open for everyone in the control room to hear. He and Dodgson began to circle each other. Security guards prepared to step in if the two men's argument turned physical.

"We are doing things here you couldn't possibly imagine," Dodgson asserted.

Ian smiled a wry, knowing smile. "I bet I can imagine some of them."

"You need to leave the premises," Dodgson ordered. "Now."

"I do," Ian agreed. "But first I owe all these folks an apology. I think by lending my cachet to this place, I might have made it seem like it wasn't rotten to the core."

"That's enough," Dodgson barked.

With Dodgson distracted, Ramsay was able to get the locations of the abandoned pod and the nearest access gate off the monitor.

"You're racing toward the extinction of our species, and you don't care," Ian said accusingly. "You know exactly what you're doing, but you won't stop."

Dodgson shook his head. "I thought you were different. But you're like everyone else. You see what you want to see."

Everyone in the room watched the conflict, mesmerized. Dodgson decided it needed to end. "Ramsay?"

Ramsay looked up from the console, startled to hear his name.

"Help Dr. Malcolm gather his things," Dodgson said. "See if you can manage to keep track of him for the entire journey this time."

Ramsay and Ian left. Dodgson looked at the video feed of the buzzing locusts in the greenhouse, and for a fleeting moment, the corners of his mouth flickered up in a nasty smile.

Making sure they weren't being followed, Ramsay and Ian hurried to a vehicle maintenance garage. Working together, they rolled out a map. Ramsay pointed to a spot. "There's an access gate at the northeast corner of the mines. If they make it out, that's where they'll be."

He grabbed a set of keys from a hanger on the wall and headed for a rugged vehicle. "You can take the service road. It'll lead you straight there."

"These roads are protected from the dinosaurs, right?" Ian asked.

"I'd drive fast," Ramsay replied.

Ian climbed in and started the engine. "You did good."

"Actually, it's a complete disaster," Ramsay said.

"Not yet," Ian assured him, shifting into gear and peeling out.

Deep in the alpine forest, Kayla stared at the blinking dot on her ejection-seat tracker. "We should be right on top of Claire," she said.

Owen looked up and saw the empty seat hanging from a branch. Its straps were open. "She got out," he said, relieved.

BOOM! The ground shook as a *T. rex* approached. Owen and Kayla hid behind a fallen tree. The *T. rex* grabbed the deer carcass left by the *Therizinosaurus* in its jaws and started to drag it away. But then a *Giganotosaurus* burst through the trees and roared at the *T. rex. ROWWAARR!*

"Allosaurus?" Owen whispered.

"Giganotosaurus," Kayla said. "Largest-known ter-

restrial carnivore. You put two apex predators in a valley, pretty soon there's only gonna be one."

Dropping the deer, the *T. rex* backed off. The *Giganotosaurus* chomped on the deer. It turned its massive head and stared in Owen and Kayla's direction. Then it tipped its head back and swallowed the deer whole. It roared again and thudded off into the woods. *ROWRRR! BOOM! BOOM! BOOM! BOOM!*

In the caves of the amber mines, Dr. Sattler, Dr. Grant, and Maisie picked their way between the stalactites. Their flashlights caught occasional reflections of crystal and moisture.

"Feel that?" Ellie asked. "An air current. There's gotta be an opening up ahead."

"How old is this mine?" Alan asked.

Ellie had no idea. "Take deep breaths. Don't panic. Watch out for bats."

"I hate bats," Maisie admitted.

"Who said anything about bats?" Alan asked nervously at the same time. He also wasn't a big fan of bats, much preferring digs on open land to excavations in caves.

"There probably aren't any," Ellie said, trying to be positive. But she couldn't keep it up. "I never should have brought you into this," she told Alan.

"What?" Alan said, surprised.

"I should have left you in your element," she said. "Where you were happy."

"Ellie," he said, finally taking his wary attention away from the idea of bats and putting it fully on Sattler. "I wasn't happy."

"You weren't?"

Maisie stared at the two adults. "Do you guys have kids?"

"Um, I do," Ellie replied. "Two. Older than you."

"Not with him?" Maisie said, meaning Alan.

"No," Ellie said, shaking her head and smiling. "We're just . . . old friends."

"Really?" Maisie said. She was pretty sure she was seeing a connection between Ellie and Alan that went beyond friendship. She might have been just a teenager, but she knew romance when she saw it—just like Owen and Claire. She thought of them and took a moment to hope they were okay.

They reached an open cavern. A ladder stretched up into a higher cave. A sliver of light penetrated the gloom. "I'll take a look," Alan said.

He climbed the ladder—watching out for bats

despite Ellie's assurances—and rested his flashlight on a rock shelf to secure his footing, but something flashed past, knocking the flashlight away.

"What was that?" Ellie asked, alarmed.

She shined her flashlight, revealing . . . a hissing *Dimetrodon,* a huge reptile that looked like a crocodile with a frilled fin three times its own height!

CHAPTER NINETEEN

Startled by the sight of the *Dimetrodon,* Alan fell, landing hard on the stone floor of the cavern. Ellie helped him to his feet. His hat had fallen off, but when he bent down to pick it up, a *Dimetrodon* ate it, nearly taking Alan's hand off in the process.

"Forget the hat!" Dr. Sattler cried. The three of them took off down a narrow rock corridor. With all its confusing twists and turns, the cave was like a maze. Shining her flashlight back behind them, Ellie saw another *Dimetrodon* chasing them.

Maisie pointed ahead, shouting, "There!" She'd spotted light—a possible exit. She, Ellie, and Alan slid past an old mining cart only to find the exit blocked by a locked gate. Ellie rattled the bars of the gate, trying to open it.

WHAM! The *Dimetrodons* pushed the rusted mining cart toward the trio, threatening to crush them against the bars.

"Help!" Ellie yelled out the gate. "Is anyone there?" Working together, she and Alan managed to engage the cart's brake so it would stop rolling toward them.

Maisie rushed to the gate and screamed at the top of her lungs. "HELP!"

A voice came out of the darkness on the other side of the gate. "Dr. Sattler?"

"Ian!" Ellie called, recognizing his voice. "Ian!"

Ian ran up to the locked gate. Noticing Maisie, he asked, "Uh, what is a child doing here?"

On the other side of the mining cart, *Dimetrodons* screeched and shrieked, trying to claw their way around or over it. "Just get us out!" Alan called desperately. "Open the gate!"

Quickly checking the locked gate, Ian found a keypad in the wall next to it. "Uh, it needs a four-digit code."

"Do you know the code?" Alan asked, struggling with the cart.

"No, I don't know the code!" Ian said.

A *Dimetrodon* snapped its long jaws inches from Ellie's hands, its teeth sparking off the metal cart. "Try something!" she screamed.

"Okay, okay," Ian said. "There are roughly ten thousand possibilities. . . ."

As the *Dimetrodons* growled and hissed from the other side of the cart, Ian tried different four-digit combinations. "Year of the moon landing. No. Miles Davis's birthday. No. My birthday. Somebody's phone number?"

"Phone numbers don't have four digits!" Maisie shouted.

"Let's all try to stay positive," Ian urged.

The cart lurched, slamming Alan up against the metal gate. He kicked a *Dimetrodon* in the face as Ian pounded away at the keypad, trying random combinations.

What Ian didn't know was that back in the control room, Ramsay had found a security camera feed that showed him what was going on at the gate. Working feverishly at a keyboard, he navigated through several screens until he was able to enter the four-digit code.

THUNK. The gate unlocked. Ellie shoved it open and dragged Maisie through. She and Alan slammed it closed just as the cart's brake failed, sending the cart crashing into the gate. The *Dimetrodons* were trapped inside. Ellie, Maisie, Alan, and Ian fell to the ground, spent.

They had no idea Ramsay had put in the code. "That was lucky," Alan said.

"It was . . . improbable," Ian agreed, amazed he'd somehow hit on the code.

"Ian," Ellie said, "this is Maisie. Charlotte Lock-wood's daughter."

"Lockwood," Ian said, remembering. "Pleasure to know you."

In the distance, they heard a spine-shivering roar. *ROAWWWRR!* "We gotta get out of this valley," Alan said.

"Mmm," Ian said, thinking. "There are research out-posts, high up and dinosaur-proof. Well, if anything's dinosaur-proof. Anyway, I say we find the closest one."

After hurrying through the valley, Claire arrived at the base of a glass observation outpost perched high in the trees. Circling the base, she found a switch labeled LADDER and flipped it, hoping a ladder would lower. It did, but unfortunately its slow descent was accompanied by a loud beeping. *BEEP. BEEP. BEEP.*

"Oh no," Claire said, afraid the sound would attract unwelcome visitors. "No, no, no."

Then . . . *CHK-CHK-CHK-CHK.* A high-pitched chittering. Claire saw a *Dilophosaurus* peek curiously around the base of the outpost. It was four feet high with two brilliantly colored crests flanking its head.

Claire stumbled back behind a tree and ducked low. But the *Dilophosaurus* tracked her. Suddenly it popped up, snapped its fan open, and hissed! Claire screamed. The *Dilophosaurus* spit venom . . . but Kayla caught the venom in her leather glove! Owen zapped the *Dilophosaurus* with Kayla's shock stick. *ZZZRT!* Hissing, the dinosaur scrambled off.

Claire rushed to Owen and hugged him. "I thought you were dead."

"Nah," Owen said, hugging her back.

Kayla pulled off her glove and tossed it into the trees. "Man, that smells bad."

RROWAARRR! Something big was roaring, and it sounded as though it was close by. "We'd better get inside," Owen said, leading the way to the metal ladder.

Night had fallen. Dodgson stood outside the greenhouse holding ten thousand engineered locusts. His head of security entered a code on a panel, and a small door opened, revealing two switches and a red button. He flipped the switches and smacked the button.

Inside the greenhouse, nozzles lowered from the ceiling. A warning buzzer sounded. *BRZZT. BRZZT. BRZZT.* Agitated, the locusts flew up, buzzing and clicking. The nozzles released flame, torching the in-sects. The locusts caught fire but didn't die, protected by their tough outer layers.

Dodgson left. The burning locusts slammed into the heavy glass roof, cracking it. *SMASH!* They broke through, swarming into the night sky.

Owen, Claire, and Kayla saw the cloud of burning insects swirling in the sky, not far off. "That doesn't seem right," Kayla said, frowning. She tried to figure out what she was looking at, this strange, glowing mass in the air.

WHOMP! A flaming insect hit the ground in front of them. *WHOMP! WHOMP!* Two more fell into a tree, setting it on fire.

As the burning swarm broke apart, locusts fell, be-coming a rain of fire.

CHAPTER TWENTY

In the Biosyn Genetics control room, shocked engineers saw reports of systems shutting down. Through the window, they could see the locust firestorm. They called for an evacuation. Denise read the announcement, broadcasting it throughout the sanctuary. "Attention, please," she read. "This is an immediate evacuation order. All employees are instructed to move to the nearest hyperloop station at once. This is not a drill."

Biosyn employees all over the complex, including Ramsay, dropped whatever they were doing and ran to the hyperloop.

Dr. Malcolm drove across the valley with Alan, Ellie, and Maisie in the all-terrain vehicle, bumping across the uneven ground. In the sky ahead, they saw the glowing swarm of burning insects. "Dodgson," Ian murmured, feeling sure he knew who was responsible.

"Watch out!" Maisie shouted.

WHOMP! A flaming locust hit the ground in front of them. Ian swerved to avoid it.

"Slow down!" Alan yelled. "There's a child back here!"

"Under the circumstances, it would be more dangerous to slow down," Ian argued, dodging more falling insects. "Is it lean into the skid or away from the skid?"

"Into!" Ellie and Maisie shouted.

"Where did you learn to drive?" Alan asked frantically.

"I didn't, technically," Ian admitted, working the steering wheel right and left. "It's just a gift."

WHOMP! WHOMP! A pair of burning locusts fell onto the open sunroof's grill. Glowing embers floated down into the vehicle. "That's bananas," Ian observed.

SMASH! A flaming insect splattered on the windshield, cracking it. Ian swerved hard, skidding to a stop at the edge of a deep ravine. The vehicle teetered over the precipice.

"Well, this seems precarious," Ian said. He checked his side mirror. "Yep. We are teetering."

"A better driver and we wouldn't be teetering," Alan said accusingly, giving his old acquaintance a surly look.

"I just saved your life," Ian said. "Where's the gratitude?"

"Can you two just shelve it?" Ellie snapped. "For once?"

Maisie looked at the three adults. "Shouldn't we all lean to the right?" They looked back at her, realizing the worth of her suggestion. They leaned to the right.

"See? This is fine," Ian said. "We're fine."

THWOMP!!! A blazing bug smacked on the hood, tipping the vehicle over the edge! It flipped and rolled, landing hard in the clearing at the base of the outpost. *WHAM!*

Maisie hung by her seat belt, upside down. Ellie and Ian were battered but conscious. Alan's eyes were shut.

"Alan?" Ellie said. "Alan?" His eyes fluttered open.

Maisie couldn't believe what she was seeing through the windshield. Over by the outpost, with fire raining down around them, were Owen and Claire! She shouted to them.

With the fire raging, it was hard to see. But Claire heard a voice. "Listen," she said. "Maisie! MAISIE!"

With her eyes full of tears, Maisie turned to Ellie and Alan. "It's my parents!"

Owen and Claire raced to the vehicle and pulled Maisie out, holding her tight. "You're okay," Claire said. "You're okay." The three of them hugged, tears running down their faces.

"Hey, kid," Owen said.

"You came to get me," Maisie said.

"Of course we did," Claire told her.

Owen and Claire looked at Ellie, Alan, and Ian. "Who are you?" Owen asked.

"Friends," Ellie answered.

"They helped me escape," Maisie explained.

"Thank you," Claire said, really meaning it.

Owen looked at Alan's bleeding forehead. "Are you all right?" Alan nodded, wiping blood away.

Kayla joined them. Maisie recognized the pilot from the airfield. "I remember you," she said.

"You too," Kayla said. She nodded toward the glass observation station. "We should get indoors." They all turned to head for the ladder.

BOOM. BOOM. BOOM.

Something big was coming. And it was close.

"Don't move," Owen and Alan both said at the same time. Everyone froze.

BOOM! A massive foot hit the ground. They all looked up to see a *Giganotosaurus* looming over them.

111

"What is that?" Dr. Sattler gasped. Even with her past experience, she was astounded by the staggering sight of the huge dinosaur in front of her.

"*Giganotosaurus,*" Alan and Kayla said simultaneously.

"Biggest carnivore the world has ever seen," Alan added.

"Bigger, bigger, bigger," Ian sighed. "Why do they always have to go bigger?"

CHAPTER TWENTY-ONE

Another burning locust fell from the sky, hitting the *Giganotosaurus* on the back. It roared with fury. Owen, Claire, Maisie, Ellie, Alan, Ian, and Kayla took advantage of the momentary distraction to slip around to the other side of the vehicle.

But the *Giganotosaurus* kept coming.

It slowly stalked the group, moving forward. Its huge tail knocked the vehicle, turning it. Trying not to make a sound, the humans had to move to stay out of sight. They couldn't hide behind it forever, though. Eventually, the enormous predator would catch them. They had to get away somehow.

Owen looked over at the ladder leading up into the observation post. Then he locked eyes with Alan. "Go," he said.

They all ran for it. Kayla quickly got to the top of the ladder, then reached back down to help Maisie.

The *Giganotosaurus* lunged toward Maisie, its teeth catching on the metal guard encircling the ladder like a tube. The guard stopped the beast's jaws from closing, but Maisie was right between the upper and lower jaw, surrounded by teeth.

"Move your feet!" Kayla shouted. "Now!"

Maisie climbed up and out just as the dinosaur ripped the metal guard off. It struggled with the twisted metal as the others scrambled up the ladder.

At the top, they tried to pry open the smooth glass panels of the observation station. The *Giganotosaurus* raised its head to their level. *WFOOO!* The animal snorted, fogging the glass around them. Then—

CLONK!

A rock hit the *Giganotosaurus* in the face. It turned and saw Ian, who had thrown the rock. Ian grabbed a sharp stick, stabbed it through the body of one of the flaming locusts, and waved it in the air, trying to scare off the *Giganotosaurus*. Or at least distract it.

CHOMP. The massive creature tried to bite the burning insect. But Ian swung it away. The dinosaur tried again. *CHOMP.* For a second time, it missed the morsel as Ian whipped it out of reach.

Ian waved the locust again, trying to keep the *Gi-*

ganotosaurus focused on it, but this time the monstrous animal didn't follow the flame. It just stared right at Ian.

"Oh boy," Ian said, knowing that wasn't good.

The *Giganotosaurus* lowered its face to Ian's level and opened its terrifying, tooth-lined mouth. Thinking fast, Ian threw the stick with the blazing locust skewered on it down the dinosaur's throat. As the *Giganotosaurus* thrashed and screeched, Ian dashed to the ladder and scurried up. His foot slipped, but Alan caught his wrist and pulled him up. Ellie and Owen helped him the rest of the way.

With Maisie's assistance, Kayla pried open one of the windows. "We're in!" she cried. Alan, Claire, and Ian followed them into the observation station. But as Owen and Ellie started to climb through the open window—

CLANK!

The *Giganotosaurus* chomped the metal balcony at the top of the ladder, ripping it away. Owen and Ellie were left hanging from the broken balcony. They tried to climb up, but the balcony kept slipping lower. The *Giganotosaurus* snapped at Ellie's feet. She kicked its snout with her boots, knocking out one of its teeth. *ROWWRRR!*

As she struggled to pull herself up, Ellie's DNA

sample pouch dropped from her belt and tumbled down the dinosaur's throat. With a burst of terrified energy, Ellie climbed up Owen's body and through the window. Owen pulled himself up just as the *Giganotosaurus* tore the balcony completely off the side of the station.

Claire and Alan pulled Owen the rest of the way into the observation outpost. "See?" Owen said, breathing hard. "Not so bad, right?"

ROOOWWAARR! The *Giganotosaurus* furiously smashed its head into the glass observation outpost and chomped on desks, chairs, and computers. Everyone scrambled toward the back wall. Claire's feet got caught in a tangle of computer cords. The raging animal pulled the other end of the tangle, yanking Claire toward its mouth. Owen and Ellie grabbed Claire's arms.

Kayla slid her shock stick across the floor to Claire, who grabbed it and zapped the *Giganotosaurus*'s eye. Roaring with pain, it withdrew and ran off into the dark.

"That got the blood going," Ian said, panting.

In the Biosyn control room, only Ramsay, Denise, and two engineers were left. Looking out the window, they saw that the animals had nowhere to go to escape from the burning valley. Ramsay decided to let them into Biosyn's research compound, which was like a massive round pen, protected on all sides. With Dodgson gone, Ramsay gave the order, and the engineers got to work shutting down the systems that kept the dinosaurs out.

Once they were down, a *Dreadnoughtus* rumbled through the massive open gate, instinctively moving away from the fires.

A pair of *Dimetrodons* plunged into the reflecting pool.

The complex was being reclaimed by nature.

While Owen found a cold pack for Grant's head, Claire checked Maisie to make sure she wasn't seriously hurt. Ian hung up the station's phone. "I can't get ahold of anyone," he said, "since everything is, you know, on fire."

Offering his hand, Owen introduced himself to Alan. "Owen Grady. I read your book on tape."

The name registered with Alan. "Owen Grady . . . you're the guy who trained raptors."

"I tried," Owen said.

Alan didn't recognize Claire. Dr. Sattler helped him out, saying quietly, "Claire Dearing. She worked at Jurassic World."

Ian overheard this. "Oh, ah . . . not in favor," he said.

"Yup, big mistake," Claire agreed.

"Terrible idea," Owen said.

Facing Ellie and Alan, Kayla asked, "So what are you doing here?"

"I needed a DNA sample from a live specimen here at Biosyn to prove they engineered those locusts," Ellie explained. "Then we could go public with the evidence and shut Biosyn down."

Alan found a smoking, charred locust on what was left of the balcony. He picked it up and set it on a counter. "Still alive," he said.

Ellie broke off a leg. *CRUNCH*. Goo seeped out.

Looking disgusted, Maisie asked, "What are you doing?"

"Science," Ellie answered simply.

"Cool," Kayla said. "You all good to find a way out of here?"

"I don't recommend the amber mines," Ian advised.

Owen grabbed a tranquilizer rifle out of a cabinet. Not the most powerful weapon, but much better than a knife.

"They've got a helicopter in the main complex," Kayla continued. "Turn the ADS back on, and we're home."

"ADS?" Alan asked.

"Aerial Deterrent System," Kayla explained. "Keeps away the nasty *Pternanodons*."

"How do we turn it back on?" Claire asked.

Maisie unrolled a map on a table.

"All systems run through the control room on the third floor of the complex. That must include ADS," Kaya said.

Owen came over to look at the map. "All these outposts are connected underground?" he asked, and Kaya nodded. Searching the round pillar in the center of the outpost, Owen found a hatch and waved Dr. Grant over. "Help me with this."

Together, Owen and Alan pried the hatch open.

"Everybody ready?" Dr. Malcolm asked.

CHAPTER TWENTY-TWO

They all climbed down a ladder to the dark hyperloop tunnel. Claire cracked a flare. They headed toward the Biosyn complex. Owen and Ian brought up the rear.

"You worked in the raptor pen," Ian remarked, appalled by the very idea.

"Yeah," Owen said.

"Inside the raptor pen," Ian said, just to be absolutely clear.

Owen kept walking. "That was the job."

In his office, Dodgson packed a thumb drive and two laptops in a briefcase. Outside, the forest was ablaze. He heard someone enter and turned to see Ramsay.

"Oh, it's you," he said. "Good. Here's what we do. ADS

is still down, so we need a hyperloop to the airfield. Don't worry—this is going to be good for us. There's opportunity in everything, even disaster." Ramsay just stared at Dodgson, who suddenly had a realization. "It was you," he said. "You told Malcolm about Hexapod Allies. Set this whole thing up."

Ramsay nodded.

"Ramsay, you were my guy," Dodgson grumbled in disbelief. "I gave you every opportunity I never had. And you do this? I wouldn't do this to my own worst enemy."

"I'm not you," Ramsay told him.

When Ian, Claire, Owen, Alan, Ellie, Maisie, and Kayla entered the control room, it was empty. Staring through the big window at the fire outside, Ian said, "This is very bad."

Claire went straight to the main control console. "Same system we used in the park."

"Could you just turn on the thing so we can leave, please?" Ian asked.

Tapping a screen, Claire quickly found the ADS setting and typed a command. Nothing happened. **ERROR 99** flashed on the monitor. "What's Error

Ninety-Nine?" she asked.

"Not enough power," a voice answered. It was Ramsay, who was standing in the doorway. "In a breakdown, all available power goes toward keeping the primary system running. ADS needs that power to reactivate."

"How can we get more power?" Ellie asked.

Sitting down at the console, Ramsay answered, "We can't. But we can redistribute what we have. All we need is to—"

"Shut down the primary system," Claire said, interrupting him. "Where is it?"

"Server room three," Ramsay said. "Next floor up."

Grabbing a shock stick and clipping it to her belt, Ellie said, "I'm going with you."

Claire picked up two radios and tossed one to Ian. "You'll give us the directions." She noticed Owen and Maisie searching the security-camera feeds. "Owen?"

One of the feeds came from a deep subfloor lined with pipes. In the live night-vision footage, Beta's eyes glowed white. She looked scared and alone. Owen tapped the monitor. "Where is this?"

Ramsay looked over. "Hydroelectric system on subfloor seven."

"Give me eight minutes," Owen said. "I can find her."

Ellie looked puzzled. "Who is this, now?"

"Beta," Maisie answered. "Blue's baby." These names meant nothing to Ellie. "*Velociraptor,*" Maisie clarified.

"A baby raptor?" Alan asked incredulously.

"I promised we'd bring her home," Owen said.

"You made a promise," Ian said, "to a dinosaur."

Grabbing a flashlight and checking his tranquilizer rifle, Owen told Maisie, "Stay here."

"No way," she insisted. "I'm going, too. She trusts me."

Owen looked at Claire to see what she thought. She was worried but decided to trust Maisie. "Okay," Claire said. "Take a flashlight."

Maisie took the flashlight from Claire, then turned to Alan. "Can you come, too?"

Having no interest in confronting a raptor, Alan hesitated. Owen said, "We could use you out there." Reluctantly, Alan nodded. Owen tossed Ian another radio. "We'll be on channel five."

"Okay," Ian said. "Any other exciting ideas?"

Claire kissed Owen and said, "Come back."

"Always do," he assured her.

Kayla grabbed a walkie-talkie off the wall and headed out. "I'll have that chopper ready to take off in ten minutes. Wait for my signal."

Kayla, Owen, Alan, Maisie, Claire, and Ellie left the

control room, leaving Ian and Ramsay to guide them over the radios to their destinations throughout the complex.

When Owen, Alan, and Maisie reached the hydroelectric power maintenance level, they stepped out of the elevator cautiously. "Maisie, hold on to me," Owen said.

Up in the control room, Ramsay called up a set of plans on the console monitor. He gave Ian directions, who passed them on to Owen. "You're almost there, buddy," Ian said. "Hundred feet past the elevator, and you'll find your dinosaur friend."

Owen, Maisie, and Alan crept down the corridor. "No sudden moves," Owen warned.

"Watch the sides," Alan added. "They always come from the sides."

Shining his flashlight, Owen spotted a makeshift nest built out of a few loose metal parts. Among the steaming pipes, he made out Beta's shadow. With his tranquilizer gun cocked, Owen stepped in front of Maisie and Alan.

Beta emerged from the billowing white steam, tense and ready to spring.

CHAPTER TWENTY-THREE

"**M**aisie, get back," Owen said in a steady voice. He aimed his tranquilizer gun at Beta. But then he hesitated, not much liking the idea of shooting the juvenile, even if it was only with a knockout dart. And if he missed, he might just make her more aggressive. He needed a clear shot.

"Go on," Alan hissed.

Beta narrowed her eyes suspiciously. Snarling, she crouched, extending her claws. *THOOMP!* Owen fired, but Beta moved incredibly fast. The dart missed its target.

Suddenly the power went out. In the darkness, their flashlights glowed in the steam. Beta stalked around them with her teeth bared, her eyes glowing like a wolf's.

The power came back. Alarm lights flashed. While Owen quickly reloaded, Alan picked up a loose wrench left behind by some worker. He knew they were being hunted, and that even a juvenile raptor could easily prove lethal.

Beta prepared to pounce. Alan raised his wrench, but Maisie stepped in between them, extending her hand. "Hey!" she yelled. Beta froze. *"Shh . . . ,"* Maisie said soothingly. "Be cool."

Stunned, Alan whispered, "She's displaying alpha confidence. And it's responding. Have you ever seen anything like this?"

"Few times," Owen said.

Beta hissed at Alan. *HISSSS!*

"Hey!" Maisie repeated. "Eyes on me." She told Alan, "She doesn't want to hurt you." Taking his cue from Maisie, Alan lowered his wrench and held one arm out with his hand flat, copying her posture.

Raising his tranquilizer gun, Owen said, "Maisie, you gotta hold her focus. Alan, spread out." Alan knew what he meant. The three humans slowly moved to form a triangle around Beta. She couldn't attack all three of them at once.

Beta looked at Owen, and then Alan. She made her choice . . . and sprang toward Alan!

THOOMP! The dart hit Beta in midair. She fell to the ground and slid to Alan's feet. "Sorry, kid," Owen told her. "I promised your mom I'd bring you home."

Claire and Ellie crept through the maze of computers in the server room. Ian's voice crackled over the walkie-talkie. "The main server is in the southeast corner. Dead ahead and to your left." Thinking of their experiences trying to survive Jurassic Park, Ian said to Ellie, "Well, here we are, together again. Makes one remember old times."

Ellie looked around the dark, eerie space. "Oh, I'm remembering them."

"Do you still have nightmares?" Claire asked her.

"All the time," Ellie said, nodding. "Do you?"

Claire looked her in the eye, as if to say "Oh yes. Lots of nightmares." Out loud she said, "I have a lot of regrets."

Ellie gave her a sympathetic smile. "When we hold on to regret, we stay in the past. What matters is what we do now. Right?"

Claire thought about that as they turned a corner and saw the floor littered with charred, half-dead locusts. They saw broken skylights. "Nobody said there'd be bugs," Claire said.

Ian's voice came over the walkie-talkie. "It's right in front of you. See it?"

Ellie and Claire picked their way through the scorched locusts. Buzzing and vibrating, the insects knocked against the two women's feet. "Insects are a natural part of our world," Ellie reminded Claire.

"Not these ones," Claire countered.

"They're more afraid of us than we are of them," Ellie assured her.

"I don't think that's true," Claire said. Finally, they reached a row of three blue computer servers lit up with green lights. "Found it," Claire said, relieved.

Ian's voice crackled through. "Okay, see that green button? Don't touch that one. That's not it. It's an ocher mustard-color button."

Claire spoke into her walkie. "They're too small. I can't see them."

"It's very simple," Ian said. "Three down from the top. No, try four up from the bottom."

"Ian," Ellie said impatiently, "we need very specific instructions."

"E seven," Ramsay told Ian. "Just say E seven."

"Okay, try the one that ends in E seven," Ian said over the walkie.

Ellie and Claire found the E7 button immediately. Claire pressed it, and the lights on the server all went out. But then they flashed on again, lighting up green one by one. "It's rebooting," Claire reported into the walkie-talkie. "It's turning itself back on!"

"Uh, it shouldn't be doing that," Ian said.

"Well, it is!" Claire said, frustrated. The rebooted system emitted a loud, high-pitched digital tone. The sound roused all the locusts, who flew up in a swarm, filling the room with their fluttering wings. Engulfed by the cloud of insects, Claire and Ellie screamed!

"No screaming, please!" Ian complained.

"ANYONE WOULD SCREAM!" Ellie yelled into the walkie. She and Claire ducked between a pair of servers, their faces and clothes streaked with ash from the locusts. With massive insects smacking into their faces, they desperately kept trying to shut down the servers. Ellie pulled out Kayla's shock stick and zapped the locusts around them. *ZZZZZTZTT!*

In the control room, Ramsay and Ian flipped through open manuals, trying to figure out how to power down the servers so that they'd stay powered down, leaving enough power for the Aerial Deterrent System. Pressing the TALK button on the walkie, Ian said, "Okay, turns out it is, uh, significantly more complex than we—"

"WE DON'T HAVE TIME FOR COMPLEX!" Ellie shouted.

CHAPTER TWENTY-FOUR

Across the room, Claire spotted a fire axe. She grabbed it, raised it high over her head as if she were chopping wood back at the cabin, and swung it down with all the force she could muster on a thick power cable. *TTZZZCCHHH!* The axe sliced through the cable. The server went dark.

Claire moved on to the next server, cutting its cable with her axe. With blue sparks flying, she hacked again and again. Smoke billowed, and the servers shut down. Claire passed the axe to Ellie, who gladly hacked away at the last cable. Finally, she cut all the way through. The last server shut down, leaving them in near darkness.

"That felt good," Ellie admitted.

"Yeah, it did," Claire agreed.

As Ellie and Claire shut down the servers, Dodgson's hyperloop pod slowed to a halt, and its glass door popped open. Clutching his briefcase to his chest, Dodgson stood and tried to pull the glass door shut, but it wouldn't budge.

He peered down the dark tunnel and spotted a light up ahead—an outpost. He figured if he could reach it, he'd be safe. But he would have to walk down the tracks of the tunnel to get there.

Treading carefully through the gloom, Dodgson heard a trilling sound behind him. *TK-TK-TK-TK-TK-TK!* He gasped and turned, dropping his briefcase. Papers, thumb drives, and laptops tumbled onto the hyperloop tracks.

TK-TK-TK-TK! Dodgson heard the trilling again. And then a second set of trills, this time from another direction, like predators calling to each other, coordinating their hunt. *TK-TK-TK-TK-TK!*

He fumbled in his pocket for his phone. When he turned on its flashlight, he saw a *Dilophosaurus* with its frill spread, vibrating! Dodgson ran back to the pod, but the *Dilophosaurus* followed, hissing. *HISSSS!*

He ran through the open pod to the escape hatch at the back, but a second *Dilophosaurus* smashed the glass. *TRSSSHHH!* Then it spit its venom right in his face. Dodgson screamed and pawed at his eyes, trying to claw away the burning goo. But when he managed to open his eyes, he saw three *Dilophosaurus* surrounding him, screeching. All three spat more gooey venom onto his skin.

Dodgson fell, and the *Dilophosaurus* began to feed.

Heading for the helicopter, Owen, Alan, and Maisie ran through the genetics lab. The room was dimly lit with emergency lighting. Owen carried Beta on his back in a sling fashioned from Maisie's jacket. The raptor was still tranquilized.

Claire and Dr. Sattler entered the lab from the opposite end. Everyone hugged, thrilled they'd all survived their missions. "You all right?" Alan asked Ellie.

"Someday," she answered.

As they turned to go, they realized there was someone lurking in the shadows.

"Don't move," Owen ordered, raising his tranquilizer rifle.

Looking exhausted and full of regret, Dr. Henry Wu stepped out of the darkness. Alan recognized him from the lab at Jurassic Park. "I remember you," Alan said. His tone of voice made it clear that this was not a fond remembrance.

"Can I shoot him?" Owen asked.

"I'm open to that," Claire said, remembering Wu's role in building the Indominus rex, the monstrous dinosaur whose escape had led to the catastrophe at Jurassic World.

"Please, listen to me," Wu pleaded. "I can set everything right. But I need her." He pointed at Maisie.

Claire stepped in front of her daughter. "No," she said firmly. "You stay away from us."

"Charlotte Lockwood used a virus to change every cell in her body," Wu said.

"We don't need a science lesson," Alan said.

"Just let me shoot him," Owen suggested.

Ellie took a step forward. "You created an ecological disaster."

Wu nodded. "Yes," he admitted. "But I can fix it. If I can understand how Charlotte rewrote Maisie's DNA, I can stop all this before it's too late."

Owen and Claire looked at each other. It was clear from their expressions that they had absolutely no intention of handing Maisie over to this man, whose efforts had already led to so much death and destruction.

"Claire," Wu begged. "You have every reason not to trust me. I've put the whole world in danger. Let me undo what I've done."

Claire's face remained stony. She couldn't forget Wu's past. But then Maisie put her hand on Owen's tranquilizer rifle, lowering it. "I want to help him," she said to her parents. She turned to Dr. Wu. "It's what Charlotte would have wanted."

Arriving from the control room, Ian and Ramsay raced into the lab. When he saw Dr. Wu, Ian said, "No, no, no, not him. It's always him."

But Wu was still focused on Maisie. "Thank you," he said.

Ian noticed Beta strapped to Owen's back. "Is that a . . . dinosaur on your back?"

"Yup," Owen responded.

"Huh," Ian said. "Well, congratulations, everybody."

Outside, Kayla descended in the helicopter, about to land on the lawn of the courtyard. Her voice came over the walkie-talkie. "I have air. Meet me at the center of the courtyard." Everyone except Ramsay hurried out of the lab, eager to escape from Biosyn Genetics.

Ramsay grabbed the walkie. "No. Do not land in here!"

"I have no choice, man," Kayla said over the walkie. "This valley isn't safe."

"They're not in the valley anymore!" Ramsay said.

From the chopper, Kayla heard a strange sound. She looked through the glass and saw a *Dreadnoughtus* appearing out of the dark. Its head was almost at the level of the cockpit. She immediately pulled up, and the dinosaur roared at the rising helicopter.

The group ran out into the courtyard, only to find themselves at the feet of the *Dreadnoughtus*. Disturbed by the chopper, the gigantic beast turned and lumbered off.

But other dinosaurs remained in the area. *Ankylosaurus* drank from fountains and pools. An *Iguanodon* nibbled leaves off a tree.

"Stay close!" Owen hissed as they raced toward the center of the courtyard. But as Kayla started to land . . .

BOOM. BOOM.

Everyone froze. The *Tyrannosaurus rex* emerged from the dark.

Seeing it, Kayla pulled up. The *T. rex* stood over the group of huddled humans, illuminated by the helicopter's bright spotlight. Alan, Ellie, and Ian stepped in front of Owen, Claire, and Maisie, preparing themselves for the worst.

But then the *T. rex* looked up. Alan turned and saw the *Giganotosaurus* approaching with its claws out. It roared at the *T. rex. RROOAARRRWWWARRRR!*

Kayla landed the helicopter in a safe spot away from the two titans. They had to get to it. "Run," Alan said.

CRASH! The *Giganotosaurus* and the *T. rex* slammed into each other. Their battle divided the humans into two groups: Owen, Claire, Maisie, and

Ramsay on one side, and Alan, Ellie, Ian, and Henry on the other. Dodging the warring giants, they all ran for the chopper.

The *Giganotosaurus* sank its teeth into the *T. rex,* sending it crashing into a stone sculpture that caught on a rock, forming a bridge. Owen, Claire, Maisie, and Ramsay were trapped underneath the stone slab with the beaten *T. rex* on it.

Ellie, Alan, Ian, and Henry made it aboard the helicopter and looked helplessly back at the four trapped under the slab. Kayla fired a white flare into the sky. The flare lit up a *Therizinosaurus* grazing on berries. The *Giganotosaurus* noticed the *Therizinosaurus* and left the *T. rex,* moving on to its next kill. Seeing their chance, Owen, Claire, Maisie, and Ramsay sprinted to the chopper and piled in. "Everybody, hang on to somebody," Kayla said as she took off into the sky.

Rain began to fall. As they looked down at the dinosaurs below, they saw the *T. rex* open her eyes. She wasn't dead! She stood up behind the *Giganotosaurus,* bit down, and drove the creature right onto the long, sharp claws of the *Therizinosaurus.* The *Giganotosaurus* was defeated.

Lightning flashed, and the *T. rex* and the *Therizinosaurus* raised their heads and bellowed at the sky. *RROOAARRWWWRRR!*

CHAPTER TWENTY-FIVE

The sun rose over the Biosyn Genetics airfield. Ian and Ramsay reported to a pair of authorities. Ramsay was saying, "Systemic corruption in the executive ranks—"

"Systemic corruption," Ian repeated. "You got that? Write it down."

Kayla was talking to a female pilot. "No, I mean they literally owe me a plane. . . ."

Alan and Ellie packed the DNA sample from the locust leg in a freezer box. "I need to have this vetted at the lab before I take it to my contact at the *Times*," Ellie told Alan. "You could come with me. Unless you have to get back to your dig."

"Ellie," Alan said, smiling. "I'm coming with you." The two doctors kissed.

Maisie saw the kiss. She looked at Owen and Claire, happy to know they were headed home together. Her parents were tending to Beta, making sure she was properly sedated for the ride back to her mother. Blue would be happy to be reunited with her offspring.

Soon they all boarded an emergency evacuation helicopter and flew away from the valley, which was still smoldering from the fire.

Days later, Dr. Henry Wu took a newly modified locust to a wheat field and released it. A massive swarm of locusts rose out of the field to meet it. With what he had learned from Maisie's DNA, he'd been able to engineer a locust whose DNA would soon spread through the locust population, rendering them harmless. The world's food supply was safe again.

Watching the locusts bob and weave above the field like a flock of birds, Henry couldn't help but laugh. It was beautiful.

On the National Mall in Washington, DC, Grant and Sattler prepared to testify before Congress. Hearings were being held to investigate Biosyn. Ramsay had served as a whistleblower, describing everything he knew about what Biosyn had been up to, including their plans to ruin their competitors with genetically engineered locusts, putting the world's food supply at risk.

Alan wasn't used to dressing in a blazer and tie. Ellie straightened his collar, telling him, "You look . . ."

"Uncomfortable," he said.

"Trustworthy," Dr. Sattler said, smiling.

"I'm getting used to it," he said, handing her back the sheaf of notes she'd given him to study before they testified.

"Okay," Ellie said, taking his hand. "Let's finish this." They headed to the Capitol.

Nearby, children had gathered at the edge of a pool, throwing bread to ducks and a few small, long-legged *Moros intrepidus*. One of the *Moros intrepidus* gently took bread from a little girl's hand. She giggled.

Coexistence with dinosaurs—to the youngest children—it wasn't strange at all. It was what they had grown up with, what they were used to.

In the Sierra Nevada Mountains, tall grass swayed in the breeze, glowing in the warm light of sunset. Claire popped the back of the truck and opened a crate. From inside, Beta hissed at her. *HISSSS!*

The grass shook. Something was moving through the tall stalks. Blue emerged cautiously from the grass, hissing, keeping her back low.

Owen, Claire, and Maisie stepped aside. For a moment, nothing happened. Then Beta bolted out of the crate and off the truck, running to her mother. The two of them danced nimbly around each other, Blue nipping affectionately at Beta's head.

Beta ran back to Maisie and circled her once as if to say, "Thank you," before running back to her mother.

Owen, Claire, and Maisie stood together, arms around each other, watching as mother and daughter retreated, disappearing into the tall weeds and grass.

But then Blue came back. She gazed at Owen. He looked at his raptor one last time, unsure if he'd ever see her again. "Go on," he said.

Blue and Beta raced off into the wild together, heading for the horizon.